The Discovery

Judy Baer

Cedar River Daydreams

1 · New Girl in Town
2 · Trouble with a Capital "T"
3 · Jennifer's Secret
4 · Journey to Nowhere
5 · Broken Promises
6 · The Intruder
7 · Silent Tears No More
8 · Fill My Empty Heart
9 · Yesterday's Dream
10 · Tomorrow's Promise
11 · Something Old, Something New
12 · Vanishing Star
13 · No Turning Back
14 · Second Chance
15 · Lost and Found
16 · Unheard Voices
17 · Lonely Girl
18 · More Than Friends
19 · Never Too Late
20 · The Discovery

Other Books by Judy Baer

- Paige
- Adrienne
- Dear Judy, What's It Like at Your House?

The Discovery

Judy Baer

BETHANY HOUSE PUBLISHERS

MINNEAPOLIS, MINNESOTA 55438

A Ministry of Bethany Fellowship, Inc.

The Discovery
Judy Baer

All scripture quotations are taken from *The Everyday
Bible, New Century Version,* copyright © 1987, 1988 by
Word Publishing, Dallas, Texas 75039.
Used by permission.

Library of Congress Catalog Card Number 92–75598

ISBN 1–55661–330-X

Published by Bethany House Publishers
A Ministry of Bethany Fellowship, Inc.
11300 Hampshire Avenue South
Minneapolis, Minnesota 55438

Printed in the United States of America

For Mom and Dad,
With Love

JUDY BAER received a B.A. in English and Education from Concordia College in Moorhead, Minnesota. She has had over twenty-six novels published and is a member of the National Romance Writers of America, the Society of Children's Book Writers, and the National Federation of Press Women.

Two of her novels, *Adrienne* and *Paige*, have been prizewinning bestsellers in the Bethany House SPRINGFLOWER SERIES (for girls 12–15). Both books have been awarded first place for juvenile fiction in the National Federation of Press Women's communications contest.

"If anyone belongs to Christ,
then he is made new.
The old things have gone;
everything is made new!"

2 Corinthians 5:17

Chapter One

Todd Winston stood in the doorway of the *Cedar River Review* workroom grinning from ear to ear.

The room, which had once been used as a janitor's storeroom, was a chaotic mess of tables, chairs, desks, and people. Every flat surface was covered with clip art and old editions of the *Review*. The bulletin boards that lined the walls were plastered with typewritten stories, clips from old papers, and black-and-white photographs.

Minda Hannaford sat on a table, one knee draped over the other, posed as though waiting for someone to take her photograph. She was lecturing Tim Anders on the merits and pitfalls of fake fur and animal-print clothing. Tim was obviously bored but too polite to interrupt Minda's lecture.

"I, of course, have animal-print accessories. People *expect* me to wear the latest fashion trends, don't you think?"

Tim rolled his eyes and nodded his head.

"I'm glad I talked to you about this," Minda concluded. "I *will* include the animal prints in my column." She hopped off the table. "It's really very important to discuss my column with someone who has a little common sense."

Tim shrugged helplessly as Minda moved to a desk to finish her work.

"I'm glad to hear you have a little common sense, Tim," Lexi teased. "I didn't realize you were Minda's new consultant on fashion ideas."

"Hey, don't look at me. I just work here," Tim pleaded. "Binky, hand me that story your brother is holding. I need a word count to see how much space it's going to take."

The paper was nearly completed and the work was winding down. Egg McNaughton didn't even notice Binky grab the paper out of his hand. He was too engrossed in a discussion with Angela Hardy.

Suddenly a sharp whistle split the air. All heads jerked toward the door where Todd stood.

"What does it take to get someone's attention around here? This place is like walking into the monkey house at the zoo."

"Wrong." Lexi walked toward Todd. "There's more organization in the monkey house."

"What's up?" Egg asked.

"It'd better be good," Minda muttered from the corner of the room. "You're interrupting me."

"I've got big news." Todd grinned at Minda. "News so big that you can afford to interrupt your column for a minute to hear what it is."

Minda laid down her pencil and folded her hands across the note pad in front of her. "Okay. I'll give you one minute."

"Watch out, Todd," Egg warned. "The last time someone interrupted Minda while she was writing her column, he ended up as a footnote in the *Cedar River Review*."

"My brother Michael is getting married!" Todd announced.

"Single-forever Mike? Taking a trip down the aisle?" Egg whistled. "That *is* news!"

Binky gave a high-pitched squeal. "Oh, that is so romantic."

Everyone was pleased by the news. The students at Cedar River High knew Mike Winston well. He ran a local garage not far from the school, and had always been willing to loan out his tools to those who wanted to tinker with their cars or motorcycles.

"Mike has always seemed so shy. I never thought he'd get around to it," Minda said. "But I'm really glad for him. He's a great guy."

"That's for sure," Tim agreed. "He's always let me use his shop to fix my car, and Matt takes his motorcycle there all the time for work. Your brother's a generous guy, Todd. I'm happy for him."

"I just love weddings," Binky chirped.

"Todd, will you be the best man?" Minda asked.

"Todd in a monkey suit?" Egg chortled. "Can't you just see it?"

In the midst of their excitement, Mrs. Waverly, the *Cedar River Review* advisor, and music teacher, walked into the room.

Binky was taking small measured steps across the room, her eyes closed, her hands clutching an imaginary bouquet of bridal flowers. She was humming softly, "Here Comes the Bride."

Egg was following his sister, making noisy smooching sounds on his arm.

Minda, who had cultivated a voice loud enough to stop traffic, yelled at all of them. "Grow up, you guys. It's just an engagement."

"Ahem." Mrs. Waverly cleared her throat. "Would someone mind telling me what's going on here?"

Todd blushed from his neck to his cheeks. "Sorry, Mrs. Waverly. It's my fault. I just told everyone that my brother is getting married."

"Why, what perfectly wonderful news! Michael was always a favorite of mine. Such a beautiful singing voice too. He was a great asset to the Emerald Tones." Mrs. Waverly referred to a select singing group that she directed, and which was her pride and joy.

"Michael was always such a quiet boy in class," Mrs. Waverly recalled. "I'm glad he's finally come out of his shell. When's the wedding?"

"I don't know. I'm not sure they know, either. He proposed to Nancy Kelvin last night. All they've been doing since is looking goofy and staring into each other's eyes."

Egg made another smooching sound on his arm.

"Exactly," Todd said. "They act like no one else in the family exists."

"What do your mom and dad have to say about that?" Binky asked.

"They're thrilled."

"Be sure to congratulate Mike for me." Mrs. Waverly tucked a yellow pencil behind her ear. "I hate to break up this engagement party, but I really do need to lock up. What's left of the paper can be finished up later. Minda, are you done with your column?"

"I'll finish it at home. It's been much too noisy in here." Minda gathered up her papers, and with a regal bearing befitting a queen, exited the room.

Tim Anders followed her. "The column can't be longer than three hundred words, Minda. If it is, we're never going to find a place for it. Minda? Are you listening to me? Minda!"

"We have a few minutes before chemistry class," Todd murmured to Lexi.

When they were alone by the lockers, Lexi took Todd's hand and gave it an enthusiastic squeeze. "Congratulations! I'm happy for Mike and your whole family. Nancy's a really nice girl." Nancy was a pediatric nurse at the hospital. She had welcomed Todd's friends into her life openly and enthusiastically.

"Mom thinks Nancy will be good for Mike," Todd confided. "She's so bubbly and full of energy, she offsets Mike's quietness and shyness. Dad, of course, thinks Nancy will be the perfect daughter-in-law, because she's interested in everything he says and does."

"She really is neat," Lexi said. "Maybe now I'll have the opportunity to get to know her even better."

"That would be good, Lexi. I think Nancy needs friends. We both know she's had some bad times in the past."

Before Lexi could respond, the bell rang, class doors opened, and students poured into the hallways.

Todd held Lexi's fingers, as if he wanted to say something.

"Remind me to give you a congratulatory kiss later," Lexi teased, "now that you're going to become a real honest-to-goodness brother-in-law."

Todd smiled. "Our family's planning an engagement celebration dinner for them tonight. Can you come?"

"Are you sure?" Lexi asked uncertainly. "I'm not family."

"Of course. You know Mike and my folks are crazy about you. So is Nancy. It wouldn't be a party without you. Nancy's parents live in South Florida, so they won't be coming to Cedar River until a few days before the wedding. Nancy doesn't have any family here."

"Then I guess I'll just have to say yes."

"Great!" Todd grinned. "You wouldn't want to miss seeing Mike act like a lovesick goofball. Last night, at three A.M., I woke up to his singing outside my bedroom window!"

"Singing?"

"I looked out, and there was Mike with a flashlight—cleaning the flowerbeds."

"Why?"

"He said he couldn't sleep. He kept thinking about Nancy and about getting married, and decided he might as well do something productive."

"So he came over to clean the flowerbeds?"

"And the garage. Then he edged the lawn and hosed down the sidewalk." Todd glanced at his watch. "Come on. We'd better hurry, or we'll be late for chemistry class."

The science lab was filling with students when Todd and Lexi entered the room. Binky sat at one end of a long black table leafing through the pages of her notebook and muttering to herself. She looked up as Lexi passed her.

"Why didn't you talk me out of this class, Lexi?" Binky demanded. "You know I'm not bright enough for chemistry."

"Bonita McNaughton, give yourself a break. You can handle chemistry as well as anyone in this room."

"Yeah, right." Binky lowered her head to the table until her forehead rested on her notebook. "I'm going to fail. I'm going to make a complete fool of myself. I will make such a *big* fool of myself that it will be written up in the *Cedar River Review*. I can see the headlines now: 'Binky McNaughton Fails Chemistry. Proves to World She Is an Idiot.'"

"Stop that, Binky," Lexi said sharply. "You're smart. All you have to do is apply yourself."

"Yeah, right. I could apply myself all I wanted and I might get a D instead of an F. I don't know the first thing about chemistry."

"You can cook, can't you?" Todd asked.

Binky lifted her head. "Huh?"

"Cooking is chemistry."

"What do you mean, 'cooking is chemistry'?"

"Baking soda does one thing in a recipe while baking powder does another. You knew that, didn't you?"

"Well, sure, but . . ."

"That's because the baking soda or baking powder creates a chemical reaction with the other ingredients in the recipe."

"Really?"

"You, of all people, have tackled some difficult cooking projects," Lexi pointed out.

"That's true, I suppose . . ."

"Remember the contest you and Egg entered?"

"You mean the one where the buns I made turned out like hockey pucks?" Binky's shoulders sagged. "I guess I don't know anything about either cooking *or* chemistry."

"Don't be so hard on yourself, Binky."

"I suppose I am a pretty daring—cook."

"Of course you are," Todd encouraged. "Just

think of chemistry like cooking. It's a challenge, that's all."

"Chemistry's like cooking, huh?" Binky chewed on her lower lip, mulling over the new concept. "Well, cooking isn't all that hard."

"Neither is chemistry. Just pay attention and take good notes."

"Yeah, yeah. I know all that." Binky waved her hand. "No sweat."

Todd and Lexi exchanged an amused glance, and moved on as Binky tackled her chemistry book with renewed interest.

"That was a good pep talk," Lexi said. "Do you think it'll work?"

"Who knows with Binky?" Todd said. "You have to be careful around her. You don't want to pep her up too much or she'll go ballistic, set up a laboratory in her kitchen, and blow the entire town off the face of the map."

"I agree, with Binky anything's possible," Lexi said. "Do you really think she could find enough chemicals to blow us away?"

"If she gets too excited, she might invent some."

"Don't forget about tonight," Todd reminded Lexi as they parted after class. "Do you want me to pick you up?"

"I'll walk over. You'll be busy getting ready for the party."

"Don't worry, I'm not cooking—whether I have an A in chemistry or not."

"I'll be there," Lexi promised. "See you then."

———

Lexi ran into the object of their discussion as she

left school for the day. Binky was standing in the school entry staring across the deserted parking lot.

"Hi, Bink. I thought you left twenty minutes ago."

"I couldn't find my notebook in my locker," Binky moaned. "I had to clean the whole thing out. I just finished putting everything back. Do you know that I found a sandwich in there from last week?"

"I don't think I want to hear about it."

"No, I guess not . . ." Binky's voice trailed away and she sighed. "I suppose that's not very interesting . . . *I'm* not very interesting . . ."

"What do you mean by that?" Lexi challenged. "You're about as interesting as any person I've ever met!"

"Then you haven't met very many people."

"What's wrong, Binky? This isn't like you. Why are you so down?"

Binky stubbed the toe of her already scuffed shoe against the concrete floor. Her shoulders drooped disconsolately, and Lexi felt a twinge of pity for her friend.

"I feel so young."

"You *are* young!"

"And dull."

"You aren't that!"

"And boring."

"What's going on, Binky? I've never seen you like this before!"

"I got a letter from Harry yesterday."

"You should be happy, not sad. Harry's a great guy and he's crazy about you!" Binky's boyfriend, Harry Cramer, was a college freshman whom Binky had begun to date in the past year.

"Maybe he *used* to be crazy about me."

"What's that supposed to mean?" Lexi thought Harry had done wonders for Binky's sometimes shaky self-esteem.

"I wish we could be together more." Binky looked as though she were about to cry. "He hardly ever comes home to Cedar River, and it's almost impossible to have a long-distance relationship."

Lexi was surprised to see tears welling up in Binky's eyes and genuine dismay written on her features. "I thought you talked to Harry every week on the phone."

"Big deal! How can I compete? I talk to him once a week on the phone. All those college girls see him every single day!"

"So *that's* what this is all about?"

Binky scowled at Lexi. "So that's what *what* is all about?"

"You're feeling insecure. It's because you're in Cedar River, and Harry is at school with a bunch of college girls."

"Wouldn't you feel the same way? He talks about his beautiful lab partner and his roommate's sister, and all these gorgeous girls he's meeting all the time. Look at me, Lexi! I'm short and stubby and underdeveloped, and ditzy besides! He's going to forget all about me!"

"Give Harry some credit, Binky. Just because he meets other girls doesn't mean he'll forget about you. I think it's neat that he tells you about his beautiful lab partner—you'd have more to worry about if he kept her a secret!"

"Maybe you're right, but I'm still afraid I'll lose him now that he's surrounded by sophisticated college girls. I just don't know what I can do to hang on to him."

"Hang on to him?" Lexi echoed. "Binky, you don't have to *do* anything. Just be yourself! You're sweet, and cute. You have a great sense of humor. Harry should be worried about hanging on to *you*!"

Binky smiled faintly. "Thanks for trying to make me feel better, Lexi. You're a real friend."

"Don't do anything stupid just because you're feeling insecure," Lexi warned. "You're great just the way you are."

"Okay—I guess." Binky didn't seem convinced. "Want to walk home with me?" she asked, trying to look cheerful.

"Sure." Lexi slung her book bag over her shoulder and followed Binky out the door.

———

"You aren't going to eat supper with us tonight?" Lexi's brother Benjamin's voice was heavy with disappointment.

"Sorry, Ben. I've been invited to the Winstons' for dinner."

"Why?" Ben asked.

"Todd's brother is getting married."

"Tonight?" Ben's almond-shaped eyes grew wide.

"No, silly. They're having an engagement party for Mike and his fiancée, Nancy. Todd asked me to join them for a family dinner."

"Can I go to Todd's house, too?" he asked eagerly. "I want to see Mike and his new wife." Ben was born with Down's syndrome. He considered the Winston family his good friends.

Lexi laughed out loud. "Mike isn't married yet,

Ben. Nancy is his *fiancée*."

"I want to see his fee-and-say. Can't I go? Please, Lexi? Please?" Lexi knew how Benjamin loved a party. "Todd would say yes. I know he would."

"Sorry, Ben. You have to stay home tonight," Mrs. Leighton said, ruffling her son's dark, shiny hair.

"But I want to go to Todd's!"

"Then who will feed your bunny, Ben? Isn't he hungry about now?"

Ben's head snapped up. "Bunny! It's suppertime." He leaped from his chair and went to the cupboard for rabbit food.

"You can take a few leaves of lettuce and a carrot too, if you want."

Ben retrieved the vegetables from the fridge. "Bye, Lexi. See you later. Say hi to Todd." Ben departed through the back door, his disappointment all but forgotten.

"I'll have to introduce Ben to Nancy sometime," Lexi said. "He'll love her. She's great with little kids."

"Sounds as though you like Nancy a great deal," Mrs. Leighton commented.

"She's just right for Mike. She's outgoing while he's shy; talkative when he's quiet; and she makes him smile."

"She sounds perfect then."

A frown creased Lexi's brow. "That's the *last* thing Nancy would say about herself. She made some bad choices when she was younger, choices that sometimes affect her image of herself."

"Everyone has some regrets in their life," Mrs. Leighton commented. "What's past is past."

"That's true. And she is determined to keep it in

the past. Nancy has only been a Christian a short time, but it's made a radical difference in her life. Sometimes when she talks about her faith she just glows." Lexi giggled as something Todd told her came to mind. "Todd says Mike acts so goofy it makes Todd want to gag at times."

Mrs. Leighton chuckled. "Young love *can* do that, if you're not the one in love. But it certainly is fun if you're the one experiencing love—especially if it's for the first time."

Mrs. Leighton's cheeks turned pink.

"Mother, are you thinking about you and Dad? What it was like when you fell in love?"

"I guess so, dear."

Lexi stood and kissed her mom on the top of the head. "I'd better sneak out now while Ben is occupied with his rabbit."

"Say hello to the Winstons for me."

"I will, if I can get a word in edgewise. I have a feeling that tonight Mike and Nancy are going to dominate the conversation!"

Chapter Two

As Lexi walked up the front steps of the Winston house, she could hear happy laughter coming from the living room. Mike Winston greeted her at the door.

"There you are, Lexi." He smiled broadly as he pushed open the screen door and pulled Lexi inside. He put his arm around her shoulder and walked her toward the living room. "I can't believe Todd didn't offer to pick you up."

"I told him not to. I thought he must have things to do around here."

"Todd? Don't kid yourself, Lexi. Mom did the cooking. Dad set the table, and I cleaned the house. My lazy little brother sat in the family room and watched TV."

"I cleaned the silverware!" Todd poked his head around the corner. "Ignore him, Lexi."

"Come on into the living room and see all the flowers," Mike said. "Mom went crazy at the florist's. I'm glad she left a few flowers for the other customers."

The room was a riot of color. Mrs. Winston stood up and greeted Lexi. "I'm so glad you could join us, dear." Mr. Winston also stood, and smiled at Lexi.

Mrs. Winston took Lexi's hands in hers and kissed her lightly on each cheek. "We're delighted you could help us celebrate Mike and Nancy's engagement."

"We definitely have something to celebrate," Mr. Winston agreed. "We will finally get this oldest son of ours married off. Someone else can worry about him for a while. Right, Nancy?"

Nancy nodded. She was seated on the sofa with her feet tucked under her and her arms wrapped around a pillow.

"Hi, Nancy," Lexi said, extending her hand. "Congratulations. When is the big day?"

"June 30th. I've always wanted to be a June bride."

Nancy motioned for Lexi to draw closer. "Come and see my ring. It's so beautiful, I can hardly stand it."

Lexi joined Nancy on the couch. Lexi had never seen an engagement ring so dazzling. "It's gorgeous!"

"Do you like it? Mike was a little worried when I told him I didn't want an ordinary engagement ring. Tell me, do you think a sapphire is too untraditional?"

"I think it's spectacular! It's the prettiest engagement ring I've ever seen."

Nancy looked at Mike from the corner of her eye. "See? I told you." She turned back to Lexi. "I informed Mike that any woman with good taste would love a ring just like this one. I'll never want another ring—except a wedding ring of course, for the rest of my life."

"When we got married, we didn't exchange rings," Mr. Winston commented. "In fact, we didn't get wedding rings until our tenth anniversary."

"Really? Why not?" Lexi asked.

"We couldn't afford it," Mr. Winston admitted. "We spent every penny we had to put ourselves through school."

"It meant some lean, hard times, but it was worth it. I'll never forget the day we went to pick out our wedding bands," Mrs. Winston remarked. "I was as excited as a brand-new bride, even though it had been ten years."

"What a nice story!" Nancy exclaimed. "I hope Mike and I have wonderful memories of our tenth anniversary."

Mike sat down on the arm of the sofa, and brushed his fingers along Nancy's forearm. Nancy looked up at him with an expression that made Lexi's throat ache.

"All right, you two, break it up." Todd entered the room with a tray of appetizers. There were bits of cheese and sausage skewered onto toothpicks, and a plate of oysters on round butter crackers.

"Todd, did you do this yourself?" Lexi asked, surprised.

"Well—Mom told me how," Todd admitted. "They aren't too bad. Here, try one." He produced a napkin from beneath the tray and handed it to Lexi. "There are crudités in the kitchen. I'll bring those in next."

"Whoa, little brother. Crudités? What does that mean?" Mike joked.

"Raw vegetables to you," Todd shot back.

"Mmmm. Why don't you call them that?"

"I'm going to have some of those—crudités," Mr. Winston said.

"And I'd better go check on the roast." Mrs. Winston excused herself.

"You work on these while I get the vegetables." Todd set the tray on the coffee table and vanished into the kitchen.

"It looks like you've all gone to a lot of work for this evening," Nancy commented to Mike.

"And you're worth every minute of it," Mike answered softly.

Lexi felt like she was intruding on their privacy. She was relieved to see Todd return with a plate of celery, carrot sticks, mushrooms, cucumber slices, and black olives.

Before long Mrs. Winston called them to dinner.

The dining room had a festive air about it. Beautiful china, crystal, and sterling silver graced the table. There were more flowers in this room—velvety pink roses in a lush display of greens and baby's breath.

"You shouldn't have done all this just for us," Nancy said, admiring the table.

"Just for you? Who is more important than our family?" Mrs. Winston said. "Why, Mike even smiles in his sleep since you've agreed to marry him. I don't know of anyone more important to save the use of our china and crystal for. And flowers add a romantic touch, don't you think?"

Tears sprang to Nancy's eyes. "Yes. And no one has ever said anything so beautiful to me. Thank you, Mrs. Winston. I can't tell you how proud and happy I am to become a part of this family."

Mrs. Winston put her arm around Nancy and squeezed her tight. "Let's sit down and say grace," she said. "Mike and Nancy, you sit on that side. Todd and Lexi, you can sit here."

Mr. Winston folded his hands and the others followed. "Dear Father," he began, "I want to especially thank you for Nancy. She has brought so much joy and pleasure into Mike's life. Bless their engagement, their marriage, and their life together. Thank you for allowing us to be together tonight, sharing our joy and giving thanks to you. Amen."

Mrs. Winston rose and went into the kitchen. She returned with a silver platter of pot roast, new potatoes, baby carrots, and pearl onions.

The meal was as delicious as it looked, but Lexi was quite certain Mike and Nancy didn't notice. They were too engrossed in each other.

Halfway through the meal, Todd prodded Lexi with his elbow. When she turned to him, he rolled his eyes.

"Todd—" Mrs. Winston warned softly.

"But Mom—"

"Are you jealous, Todd?" Mike asked teasingly.

Lexi put her hand to her mouth to stifle a giggle. It was different to see Mike so utterly lovesick.

It was Nancy, however, who had Lexi's full attention. It had been several weeks since Lexi had seen her. Nancy was normally robust, athletic-looking. Lexi remembered her home being cluttered with skis, tennis racquets, and various other pieces of sports equipment. Tonight, Nancy looked as if she'd lost several pounds. She was thin and pale.

"More roast beef, Nancy? Another potato perhaps?" Mr. Winston passed the platter.

"No, thanks. It tasted wonderful, but I'm full."

"Full? On those few bites? Come on, dear, you need your strength to make wedding plans," Mrs. Winston offered.

"Maybe one small slice of roast beef," Nancy conceded. She took such a tiny sliver of meat it was hardly noticeable on her plate.

"That should really pump up strength, Nancy," Todd quipped.

"Don't tease," Mrs. Winston chided. "If she's not hungry, she's really normal. I lost ten pounds before my wedding day."

"Was it because you were in love or because you wanted to fit into your wedding dress?" Mr. Winston teased.

"That's it! Nancy's already bought her wedding dress and she thinks it's too tight," Todd rejoined. "Well, don't diet for my brother's sake. You look perfect just the way you are."

Nancy burst out laughing. "Why, Todd, how sweet of you!" She held her hand over her flat stomach. "I think your mother's right, though. It's pre-wedding jitters. Now that we've decided to get married, I have a million things to think about. Who has time for food?"

Mike did not join into Nancy's lighthearted chatter. His expression was serious. "You *are* losing a lot of weight. Maybe you'd better quit dieting."

"But I'm *not* dieting," Nancy insisted. "I'm just not hungry these days."

"You haven't been letting my brother cook for you, have you?" Todd asked. "That could ruin your appetite. You should let Mom feed you. She'll fatten you up in no time."

"You're all very sweet to be so concerned," Nancy assured them all, "but I'm just fine. There's a lot to think about now. Besides, I haven't cut back on my hours at the hospital. I should ask for fewer hours until after the wedding, but I love to be at work. If I take time off, I'll miss my babies."

"You don't want to get run-down, Nancy," Mrs. Winston said.

"Mom's right. You should pay more attention to yourself," Mike chided. "You're always so worried about your patients at the hospital that you tend to take your own health for granted."

"I'll tell you what," Nancy said, "when we have our blood tests for our marriage license, I'll talk to the doctor. I'll tell him that you're all concerned about my health. He'll probably say that I'm marrying into a very concerned and loving family, but that there's no reason to worry. As soon as this wedding is over, I'll start eating normally again."

"Tell me about your wedding plans, Nancy," Lexi encouraged. "What have you done so far?"

"Actually, we haven't come to an agreement yet about whether it will be a small wedding or a large one. Mike is voting for small, but I'd like a huge one." Nancy clapped her hands and laughed. "Mike's asked Todd to be the best man, of course. And a close friend of mine from work will be my maid of honor. And you should see my dress. It is *so* beautiful!"

"You have your dress already?"

"Purely by accident. This morning I went into a bridal shop to look around, and there it was—hanging on a mannequin in the center of the store. I knew the moment I saw it that it was *my* wedding dress. It's ivory, with tons of little pearls sewn all over it. It could have had 'Nancy's dress' embroidered across the bodice; it is so perfect for me."

"What do you think of it, Mike?"

"The first chance I'll get to see that dress is when she walks down the aisle."

"That's another thing that's taken care of," Nancy said. "I reserved the church for the wedding and the reception. Then I turned the reception plans over to my mother. She's already been on the phone to the caterers planning fancy little sandwiches and cookies the size of your thumbnail. I'll order the wedding cake. Other than that, the reception is in Mom's very capable hands."

"Are you having a flower girl and a ring bearer?" Lexi asked.

"I don't know. We haven't ironed out all the details yet."

Lexi's thoughts drifted toward the future. What would it be like, she wondered, to be the one getting married? Thrilling? Exciting? Scary?

She smiled secretly to herself. Would it be Todd that she would marry? There were a lot of years ahead before that question could be answered. What's more, that was a question Lexi intended to leave in God's hands. She'd know when the time was right—just as Mike and Nancy had.

Mike's voice interrupted her daydreams.

"But I do know where we're going on our honeymoon."

"Where?" Todd leaned forward.

"Nowhere that I'll ever tell you about, little brother."

"You're no fun."

"Do you know where you'll be living?" Lexi asked.

"The lease on my place is up two weeks after our wedding," Nancy said. "We'll live in Mike's apartment when we return from the honeymoon. We can take our time looking for a house."

"Looking for a house sounds like fun," Mrs. Winston remarked.

30

"I want to get one that's not too small. After all, we're going to need plenty of space, and a big yard with plenty of room for children, dogs, cats . . ."

"Nancy's menagerie," Mike explained.

"She's right. I wouldn't want my grandchildren to be crowded," Mrs. Winston teased.

By the time the meal was over, everyone was laughing and enjoying one another's company.

After a short time of visiting in the living room, Lexi rose to leave. "Thanks a lot for everything. I really appreciate being invited and included in your family party."

"And we're awfully glad you could come," Mrs. Winston said.

After goodbyes were said to all, Todd walked Lexi to his old '49 Ford Coupe.

Inside, Lexi leaned her head against the seat and sighed. "Isn't it wonderful, Todd?"

"What's that?"

"Mike and Nancy's engagement and wedding plans," Lexi said. "It's so romantic."

Todd chuckled. "You sound like Binky."

"You know what I mean. They're so much in love. The wedding, the honeymoon, plans for a first house with a yard big enough for kids and pets—it all sounds perfect to me."

"You're right, Lexi." Todd's expression was thoughtful. "It does sound perfect. I can't think of a couple who deserves it more."

"Lexi, the telephone is for you!" Benjamin called from the bottom of the stairs.

Lexi sighed and closed her chemistry book. It had

been a long night of studying, and she was glad for a diversion. She was surprised, however, to hear that Binky was calling her this late.

"Hi, Bink, what's up?"

"Oh, Lexi, it's started! I know it has. I *told* you this would happen!"

"Slow down. What's wrong?" Lexi was alarmed by the panic in Binky's voice. "Is something wrong with Egg?"

"Egg? What does he have to do with this? He thinks I'm being stupid, but I'm not. I had a *feeling* about this. A *bad* feeling. And now I have proof!"

"*What* are you talking about?"

"Harry, of course!"

"Oh. I thought something terrible had happened to someone in your family."

"Something *has* happened, Lexi. Harry is dating someone!"

Lexi sat down hard on the chair behind her. "You're kidding!"

"Would I kid about something as serious as that?"

Lexi could hear the sound of crinkling paper. "I've got his letter right here, Lexi. He wrote to tell me that he's been going out on dates with his lab partner. He said he didn't want to keep any secrets from me because he knew that would hurt me. Didn't he realize how much the *truth* would hurt?"

"Slow down, Bink. Tell me exactly what Harry said."

"I'll read his letter to you. You'll see what kind of scum he is!" Binky began to read in a voice that trembled with anger and frustration:

Dear Binky,

    Sorry it's taken so long for me to write. I've been having a rough time in biology and doing lots of extra studying. I think I'm going to pass, thanks to the help of my lab partner, Mary. We've been going to the library every night for the past two weeks and really hitting the books. Mary has been great. I took her out for dinner last night just to say thanks for the help she's given me.

    I haven't had much time for socializing, but did go to a movie with Jill, a girl I met in my history class. It was great to get off campus and relax for a few hours.

    I don't mean to upset you, but I wanted you to know about Mary and Jill. I know we don't keep secrets from each other, so I thought I'd better tell you about them. I'd hate for you to hear from someone else that I'd been studying every night with another girl. Don't worry about it. It's no big deal. They're just friends.

    I really miss you, Binky. I wish you were here to study with me. You make me laugh like no one else can.

                      Love, Harry

Binky's voice was still quavering when she finished the letter. "See? What did I tell you? He's been with another girl every night for the past two weeks!"

"They've been studying, Binky. That doesn't mean they're *dating*."

"Yeah, right. Get real, Lexi. You know exactly what it means."

"He said it was no big deal. And at least he told you. If he were serious about either of these girls, I doubt he would have mentioned them to you."

"Maybe he's not serious *yet*, but he will be. How could he help it? I'm stuck in Cedar River and he's off at college! I can't really say I blame him. It makes sense that he'd want to be with people his own age—especially girls. We agreed when Harry went to college that it would be all right to see other people. I just didn't know it was going to be so hard."

"Look at it this way, Binky, Harry's being totally up front and honest with you. He cares about you. When he comes home for a visit, you two will have to sit down and discuss the situation."

"Terrific. Now instead of looking forward to seeing him, I'll be dreading a discussion."

"Don't be so negative. Maybe things will work out just fine."

"I doubt that, Lexi—unless I can figure out a way to hang on to Harry when all those college girls want him."

"There you go again!" Lexi blurted in frustration. "Harry is a person, not a possession. Don't twist yourself into knots trying to keep him loyal to you. If he's not bright enough to see what a good thing he has in you, then he's not worth bothering about."

"Thanks for trying to make me feel good about myself. I appreciate the effort."

"Did it work?"

"Not exactly."

"Oh, Bink, don't sell yourself short. You're a great person. Someday you'll find the perfect guy. If it's not Harry, so what? We're sixteen! It's no big disaster if it doesn't work out with you and Harry."

"You're so practical," Binky sighed. "I think with my emotions. I wish I were more like you."

"I wouldn't change anything about you, Bink. Not one sweet, quirky thing."

"Thanks for listening," Binky murmured.

"Anytime."

Lexi was pensive as she hung up the telephone. She hoped Binky and Harry could straighten things out before Binky did something she'd regret.

Chapter Three

"Egg, if you want more popcorn, you're going to have to make it yourself," Todd announced as he handed his friend a third huge batch. The gang was gathered at Todd's house after school.

"This should be fine," Egg said cheerfully.

"As long as nobody else wants some." Binky poked her hand into the fluffy yellow corn and helped herself. "Jennifer, Peggy, Lexi, do any of you want some before my garbage-disposal brother finishes it off?"

"No thanks."

"None for me."

Binky gazed vacantly at the popcorn in her palm until Lexi waved a finger in front of her nose. "What are you thinking about? Is popcorn that interesting?"

"Huh? Oh no." Binky blinked rapidly. "I was just thinking."

"News bulletin. 'Binky McNaughton Thinks.' That should hit all the evening papers," Egg said sarcastically.

"Quit teasing her, Egg," Lexi chastised. "What were you thinking about, Binky?"

"I was thinking how much popcorn kernels are like rice. And rice made me think about weddings, and weddings made me think about Mike and Nancy's."

"Aren't you sorry that you asked?" Egg said. "Binky's train of thought is more like a maze."

"Leave her alone, Egg," Jennifer Golden ordered. "I want to hear about Mike's wedding."

"Me, too," Peggy Madison chimed. "Tell us about the wedding, Todd."

Lexi had a hunch there was a great deal more on Binky's mind than popcorn and rice—like Harry Cramer, for example—but this was no time to bring up that particular topic.

"I can't tell you everything about their wedding plans," Todd said, "but I can tell you the most important part—I'm the best man."

"Good going."

"The term is a little deceptive," Egg said. "If *I* were going to be the best man, that would be truth in advertising. Since Todd's going to be best man, it means that a fair-to-average guy is standing in for the best man."

"Listen to the smart aleck!" Binky blurted. "You are *not* funny, Egg."

"Egg's just jealous because he's not going to be the best man," Todd offered.

Egg shook his head violently. "Not for a minute. Todd, are you going to have to wear one of those penguin suits?"

"A tuxedo, you mean?"

"That's what I said. A penguin suit."

"I suppose so. Nancy says my brother has to wear one. And if he has to, I know he'll make me do the same."

"Misery loves company."

"I think men in tuxedos look very handsome." Jennifer batted her eyelashes at Todd. "Lexi, you'd better watch out. All the girls at the wedding will be falling in love with Todd in his tuxedo."

"They'll still look like penguins to me," Egg muttered.

Binky poked him with the corner of her chemistry book. "What do you know, Egg? You have no taste."

"I have more taste on the tip of my tongue than you have in your whole mouth."

"Hah!"

"Hah!"

"What would those two do with their free time if they couldn't spend it bickering with each other?" Peggy asked Lexi as they watched Egg and Binky torment each other.

"What would *we* do if we didn't have Egg and Binky to entertain us? That's the other question."

"True. We have our own built-in comic relief. That's better than having our very own fashion consultant," Jennifer remarked, referring to Minda Hannaford.

"What time is it?" Todd glanced at his watch. "After five already?"

Egg looked at his watch. "About fifteen after."

"I wonder where my folks are? Usually one of them is home by now."

"Maybe they got stuck in traffic," Binky offered.

"Binky, we don't have enough traffic in Cedar River to get stuck in."

"Oh, yeah. I keep forgetting." Binky returned to her chemistry book. "Chemistry is getting to my brain."

"Well, at least *something* is," Egg said with a grin.

Binky looked like she was about to knock Egg over the head with her chemistry book when the telephone rang. Lexi held a finger to her lips. "Shhhh."

"Hello, Winston residence ... No, Mike's not here. Did you try the garage?" Todd fell silent.

Lexi saw Todd's expression change from relaxed to tense. When he replaced the receiver, his features showed real concern. "Todd? Is everything all right?"

"That was Nancy's friend from work on the phone. She's looking for Mike."

"Why didn't she call the garage?"

"She did. Ed told her Mike was test-driving a new car for my dad. I'd forgotten about it. Dad's looking at a secondhand vehicle and he wanted to be sure it was in good shape before he bought it." Todd looked pale, and he gripped the back of a straight chair until his knuckles were white.

"Is something wrong?" Lexi asked.

"Nancy's in the hospital."

"Of course she is," Binky said. "She's a nurse; she's always in the hospital."

"No, I mean she's a *patient* in the hospital."

"What's wrong with her?" Jennifer asked, her voice showing alarm.

"She has pneumonia—a strange variety. Pneu-mo-cys-tis, or something."

"Sounds weird."

"How'd she get pneumonia?"

"Why does anyone get sick, Binky?" Egg turned to his sister.

"Nancy's friend sounded really nervous," Todd said, his head down.

"I hope it's not too bad," Peggy said.

"Shouldn't we be doing something?" Binky asked. "Like trying to find Mike?"

The sound of a car pulling into the driveway diverted everyone's attention.

Todd looked startled to see his brother walk through the door.

"Hi, guys. Did I interrupt a study session?" Mike looked at the closed books and somber faces. "A big test tomorrow or something? Why is everyone so gloomy?"

"Mike, one of Nancy's friends called here looking for you."

"Oh, why?"

"Nancy has been admitted to the hospital. She has pneumonia."

Mike looked as though his knees would buckle. Todd took a step forward and grabbed his brother's arm. "Are you okay?"

"I've got to get to Nancy." Mike shook off Todd's grasp. "If she calls, tell her I'm on the way to the hospital. Todd, I'll need to take your car. Can I have the keys? I'll leave the one I test drove for Dad. Tell him not to buy it; it's a lemon." Todd handed Mike his keys, but before he could say anything, Mike bolted out the door and down the steps.

A few moments later, Todd's mom returned home. Mrs. Winston dropped her briefcase onto the loveseat in the foyer and came into the living room.

"Todd, did you get a call . . ."

"Mike's already left for the hospital."

"Apparently Nancy is very ill." Concern was etched on Mrs. Winston's features. She ran her fingers through her hair distractedly. "I hope Mike calls as soon as he knows something."

"She must have become sick quickly," Peggy said.

"It does seem that since their engagement, Nancy has gotten thinner and paler. We've attributed it to pre-wedding jitters, too many hours at the hospital . . . but I never expected this! I'm very worried about her," Mrs. Winston said. "Very worried."

Lexi had a bad feeling in the pit of her stomach. Tonight she would remember Nancy and Mike in her prayers.

"Lexi, have you heard anything about Nancy?" Binky said first thing at school the next morning.

"Nothing. I talked to Todd last night, but all he said was that Mike was still at the hospital."

"Poor Mike and Nancy," Binky said sympathetically. "What a bummer for her to get sick right now. Just when they're planning the wedding."

"How are *you* doing, Binky?" Lexi asked softly. "I've been worrying about both you and Nancy."

"I'm okay." Binky shrugged. "I try not to think about it. It drives me nuts imagining Harry with another girl, but I guess I should have expected it. I'm just an unsophisticated high-school student. What makes me think I can do anything to attract a college guy?"

"It's Harry we're talking about, Binky. He's your friend. You don't have to do or be anything except who you are!"

"I'm not sure about that anymore, Lexi. To keep Harry Cramer interested in me, I have to be *special*."

"You *are* special."

"Oh, Lexi, you don't understand!" Tears pooled in

the corners of Binky's eyes. "I don't want to lose Harry, but I feel so helpless . . ."

The bell rang at that moment, sending Lexi and Binky to their respective classes. Lexi had a hard time concentrating, however, and was relieved when choir practice rolled around. If Mrs. Waverly couldn't take Lexi's mind off her friends' problems, no one could.

Ultimately, it was not Mrs. Waverly who distracted Lexi, but Minda.

"What are you wearing today, Minda?" Jennifer asked when Minda strutted into the room.

"It's the Western look. How do you like it?" Minda pivoted on the toes of her cowboy boots, displaying a denim skirt and a top made from a Western blanket. She wore silver and turquoise earrings and a cowboy hat.

"Did you hitch your horse outside in the parking lot?"

Minda glared at Jennifer and turned her nose in the air. "You people have no sense of style. This is a very hot fashion trend. Get used to it, because you're going to see a lot of it."

"In other words, *you* have a lot of it. Is that what you're saying?" someone asked.

"All right, people," Mrs. Waverly interrupted smoothly. "Minda, you look very nice. Now sit down, and get out your music."

Even though Mrs. Waverly had chosen some of Lexi's favorite music, she couldn't concentrate. By the end of the hour, Lexi was simply mouthing the words. It was too easy to see the worry and concern in Todd's expression, and to remember how thin and pale Nancy had looked at the engagement dinner.

Lexi couldn't keep her mind on anything.

Todd caught Lexi in the hallway as they left the classroom. "Have you got anything going on after school tonight?"

"Nothing special. Just a lot of homework."

"Would you go to the hospital with me? I want to see Nancy, but I don't feel like going alone."

"Do you think it would be all right? Do they want her to have visitors?"

"I don't know," Todd said. "I haven't talked to my brother since Nancy got sick, but I think I should make an effort to visit her. If we don't get to see her, at least Mike will tell her we've been there."

"If you think it's a good idea . . ."

"I figure if Nancy doesn't want visitors or can't have them, Mike needs the company. I feel I owe him that much."

"All right. I'll go."

"I'll meet you by the lockers after school," Todd said.

———

The rest of the day was lost to Lexi. No matter how hard she tried, she couldn't think of anything except Nancy and Mike.

Later, as Todd drove toward the hospital, Lexi knew he was nervous by the way he tapped his fingers against the steering wheel, and by the way he drove. "Slow down, Todd. There's no hurry."

"Sorry. I have a really bad feeling about this."

"Just because Nancy has pneumonia doesn't mean she and Mike won't be getting married, Todd."

Todd ran his fingers through his wheat-blond hair. "I know it sounds dumb, but I have this feeling

. . . I can't explain it." He glanced sharply at Lexi. "Nancy didn't look very good at our place the other night, did she?"

Lexi could hardly deny Todd's assessment. "Not as good as she has looked in the past. But she's got a lot on her mind. Her job is very stressful, and she has a wedding to plan."

"I know, but she said her mom is doing the whole reception. What else is there? It just doesn't *feel* right—her being so sick. Maybe I'm just worried for Mike, because I've never known him to be in such a panic before."

"Maybe you've just never seen him in love before," Lexi pointed out softly.

Todd pulled into the parking lot nearest the front door of the Cedar River Hospital. The yard was well-groomed. Warm yellow lights were visible in several windows. Lexi shuddered. The place brought back memories of Todd's long stay here after his football injury. She could tell by his expression that he was remembering, too.

They walked through two sets of glass double doors and into the waiting room. To the left was the information desk, and straight ahead were rows and rows of bright blue and orange chairs. Lexi noticed a small gift shop to her right, the display window filled with balloons, flowers, and candy.

Todd followed Lexi's gaze. "I should have brought her something. I was in such a hurry to get here I didn't even think of it."

"Maybe we can find a gift here." Lexi took Todd's hand and drew him into the shop. "What do you think she would like? A book? A tape, maybe?"

"There's not much here that Nancy would be interested in," Todd finally concluded.

"How about this?" Lexi picked up a pink teddy bear. There was an embroidered heart on his stomach with the words "Love is a Teddy Bear."

"Good idea." Todd took the bear and set it on the counter. He pulled out his wallet and laid a twenty-dollar bill next to the bear. "I'll take it." While the cashier rang up the sale, Lexi returned to the hallway.

Why was it, she wondered, that hospitals all smelled the same? It was an antiseptic odor that always seemed to stick in her throat. She was relieved when Todd was ready to find Nancy's room.

They went to the information desk, where a pleasant-looking woman with ruddy cheeks and ample bosom informed them that Nancy's room was on the third floor.

The elevator ride was swift and smooth. When the doors opened, Lexi and Todd could see Mike at the end of the hallway, pacing in front of a large window.

Rays of late afternoon sun streamed through the window. Mike looked like a dark shadow in a black shirt and jeans.

"He looks awful," Lexi whispered.

"He hasn't combed his hair or shaved for two days, that's why. I would never have suspected Nancy's illness would affect him like this. He's usually so laid back. He was like a rock when I was in the hospital. Even when the doctors were saying I could be paralyzed, he was so calm and collected he made me feel like everything would be all right."

"Well, he's not calm now," Lexi observed.

"He and Nancy are really dependent on each other. Until Mike met Nancy, I think he'd given up on falling in love."

"Why do you think that?"

"Because he's so quiet and shy, I think he assumed it just wasn't going to happen for him. It was pretty much the same for Nancy. Because of her life before she became a Christian, she didn't consider herself worthy of finding someone who would really love her."

When Todd and Lexi approached, Mike looked up.

"What's *really* wrong with Nancy?" Todd asked when they were closer.

Chapter Four

Mr. and Mrs. Winston came down the hallway just as Todd spoke.

"Todd, I'd like to talk to you and Lexi alone," Mrs. Winston said softly, leaving no room for argument. "Mike, will you excuse us?"

Mike turned away. "Of course. As soon as the nurse comes out of Nancy's room, I'll be going back in to be with her." Mike's full attention was focused on the closed door in front of him.

"We can talk in the family room," Mrs. Winston said, leading Todd by the arm. Lexi followed, and Mr. Winston closed the door behind them.

The room was without windows, but looked comfortable enough with several lived-in-looking couches and chairs. There was a TV mounted on the wall, and end tables were strewn with magazines. At the back was a small kitchenette, with fresh coffee brewing in the coffeemaker.

"This is where we've spent most of our time," Mrs. Winston began. "There is even a bathroom with a shower." She pointed to a closed door in the corner. "Mike has slept here at least one night."

Todd grabbed his mother's arm. "Mom, can you just tell us what's going on?"

"Of course. Would you and Lexi please sit down?"

Lexi felt a cold rush of fear sweep over her. Mrs. Winston was an attractive woman, but today she looked like a porcelain doll—fragile, and ready to shatter.

Mr. and Mrs. Winston took seats on the couch across from them. "As you know, Nancy has pneumonia."

"I know that, Dad. But they can cure pneumonia, can't they?"

Mr. Winston nodded. "Nancy has a particular kind of pneumonia, called *pneumocystis carinii*. Normally it is found in people who take drugs to suppress their immune systems in preparation for surgical transplants. It is also found in cancer patients."

"Are you saying Nancy has cancer?"

"No. No, she doesn't have cancer."

"Then what is it?"

"Nancy has AIDS." Mrs. Winston's hands trembled, and a shocked silence fell over the room.

Finally, Todd spoke again. "AIDS?"

Nancy? AIDS? How can it be? Suddenly the school lectures that had seemed distant and unrelated to Lexi's life became very real. Lexi wished she'd listened more closely. It never occurred to her that someone she knew or loved might ever be touched by this terrible virus. Now, here she was, sitting in the family room of the Cedar River Hospital trying to comprehend the enormity of the Winstons' announcement.

Todd seemed to be having an even more difficult time understanding what his parents were telling him.

"There's got to be some mistake. The doctors

probably mixed up the test results. They're wrong; I know they are."

"Todd, the doctors are sure," Mr. Winston said evenly.

"No." Todd shook his head, his expression determined, unbelieving. "It's got to be wrong. It's all wrong."

"The doctors are doing another blood test tomorrow. No one wants to make any mistakes," Mrs. Winston consoled.

"It's not possible, Mom. You know Nancy." He paused. "You know the way people contract AIDS."

"Todd, I understand what a shock this is to you," Mrs. Winston murmured. "I feel exactly the same way. I never dreamed, not in a million years, that someone in *my* family could contract AIDS."

"Mike! What about Mike . . ." Todd's question broke off.

"That's the first question I had to ask," Mrs. Winston admitted.

Lexi felt as though she were eavesdropping on a conversation too personal and private for her to even be in the room, but Mrs. Winston continued.

"Mike has assured me that he and Nancy made a decision early on to wait until after marriage to have any sexual relations. He believes there's no way he could be infected." Mrs. Winston looked directly into Todd's eyes. "Abstinence before marriage is what God intended. In this instance, it probably saved Mike's life."

"How could she *do* this to us?" Todd's anger and frustration spilled over. "I can never forgive her for this!"

Mrs. Winston closed her eyes and rubbed her forehead. "Todd, I realize you are upset and angry. But your anger isn't going to help right now. We all have to get through the next few days as best we can. Lashing out at Nancy isn't going to help."

"Nancy is scared, hurting, and confused," Mr. Winston continued. "Her family is far away. That makes it more important than ever that we help her through this difficult time. Your brother loves her. We love her. Now we've got to put that love into action and be there for her when it counts."

"I'm trying to believe this is true, but I can't." Todd shook his head stubbornly. "It doesn't make any sense."

"Todd, you're going to have to accept it." Mr. Winston sounded firm but sad.

"But Nancy's so healthy and athletic. She can run circles around Mike in almost any sport she chooses."

"Denial isn't going to help, son."

"Everybody's concerned because she's lost a little weight, that's all. It's no big deal. She's thinner than she used to be. She has pneumonia. People recover from that. She's a healthy person."

"Todd, the weight loss is only one symptom . . ."

"Don't people with AIDS look sick?" Todd kneaded the sofa cushion with his fist. "I don't see how Nancy can have AIDS and not look sick."

Lexi reached for Todd's hand, but there was no response. Lexi couldn't blame him. Her own anxiety was overwhelming.

"It's impossible to tell if someone is infected with the disease by how they look," Mr. Winston explained.

"But if a person has AIDS, they *are* sick. Right?"

"Not always," Mr. Winston continued. "Not at

first, anyway. That's why it's such a hazardous disease. People can look healthy and still carry the HIV virus that causes AIDS. Sometimes teenagers, college students—even wonderful people like Nancy—at some point in their lives make the critical decision to become intimate with someone they don't know well."

"Is that how Nancy got this disease? Through sex?"

"Very likely," Mrs. Winston answered. "But now is not the time to ask that. We have to surround Nancy with our love and support, whatever comes next."

"And what *does* come next?"

"For now, all Nancy's energy must be channeled into battling the pneumonia. I'm asking both of you not to mention to anyone the fact that she has AIDS. We've only told you because Nancy insisted. She wants you to be there for Mike, Todd. And she knows what a dear friend you are to both Todd and Mike, Lexi. You'll have to support one another. But we must agree that it's Nancy's decision as to when and if she tells anyone else about her disease."

Mrs. Winston stood and reached for Todd's hand. "We've got to be strong for Nancy." Todd came to his feet and embraced his mother.

"I have to go to Mike now," Mrs. Winston said softly. "I know how difficult it is for you to hear this, both of you." She looked at Lexi, then Todd. "Your dad and I will be right outside if you need us."

When they were finally alone, Todd opened his arms and Lexi fell into his embrace. Her tears came freely. It felt good to cry. When she realized Todd was sobbing, too, she thought her heart would break.

Lexi had only been home a few minutes when Binky arrived on her doorstep, looking agitated.

"Binky, hi. Listen, I'm really exhausted tonight, so if you don't mind . . ."

Ignoring Lexi's subtle plea, Binky pushed her way into the house. "I've got to talk to you. Something has happened and I don't know what to do."

Lexi sighed. This seemed to be a night for trouble. "Come on in. I'll make some popcorn."

"I can't eat. I nearly threw up after supper." Binky headed straight for the couch and flung herself across it dramatically. "I'm losing my mind."

"Your brother Egg tells you that all the time," Lexi reminded Binky gently, hoping a little humor would cajole her friend out of her strange mood.

"This isn't funny, Lexi. This is *serious*."

"Then you'd better tell me about it." Lexi curled up on the chair across from Binky, fighting her own exhaustion and depression.

"Harry called me tonight."

"That's good. I knew he wouldn't forget about you. Don't you feel better?"

"He asked me to visit him at college."

"Even better! He can introduce you to all his friends—including his lab partner. Then they won't seem so intimidating . . . Binky, why are you looking so strange?"

"Harry said his roommates will be gone the weekend I come."

"That's too bad. You'd probably like to meet them too . . ."

"Lexi, don't you *get* it?"

"Get what?" Didn't Binky want to see Harry? What more did she want?

"He invited me to stay with him in his dorm room!"

Silence fell between them, until they could have heard a pin drop.

"What did you say?"

"Harry invited me to visit him at college and stay with him in his dorm room," Binky repeated evenly.

"But you can't do that!"

"Can't I?" Binky rolled to her side on the sofa and averted her eyes so she wouldn't have to look at Lexi. "Maybe this is the answer to all my problems. I've been worrying that Harry will forget about me while he's away at college. If I stayed with him for a weekend, it would be a lot harder for him to do that."

Lexi gasped. "I can't believe you are saying this, Binky. Are you crazy? You and Harry—alone—sleeping together in his dorm room? Do you know what that could lead to?"

"I'm not stupid," Binky muttered. "I don't really think anything would happen, but . . ."

"But if it did . . . Harry would feel committed to you and would forget about those other girls. Is that it?"

"Something like that."

"Who says Harry *would* forget about those girls? Maybe he'd be embarrassed that the two of you were intimate and forget about *you*. Did you ever think of that?"

"Lexi, that is highly unlikely. I don't think that could happen."

"That's because you're not thinking, period! Why would you even consider putting yourself in such a potentially dangerous situation? Binky, sex is nothing to be taken lightly. It's meant for two people who love each other and who are married to each other."

"I think I love Harry."

"Great. That sounds like a perfect reason to do something stupid," Lexi said sarcastically. "Binky, where is your brain?"

Binky groaned and rolled onto her back. She gazed at the ceiling. "I don't want to sleep with Harry, not really. I just don't want to lose him. If I don't sleep with him, what if one of those other girls does? What will happen then? He'll break up with me for sure."

"If he sleeps with another girl, you shouldn't *want* him as your boyfriend."

"It's easy for you to say, Lexi. You have Todd. He's a Christian, like you are. You both know that you want to wait for marriage. I'm not sure that I'm brave enough to tell Harry that I don't want sex to be a part of our relationship."

"But you *are* brave enough to have sex with him? Give me a break! That's how girls get pregnant. That's how they get AIDS. It seems to me that either you have to be really brave or really foolish to risk that."

"But you're so strong, Lexi."

"And so are you. What about the things you've learned since you became a Christian? Premarital sex is wrong. That's not part of God's plan for us. Don't do something foolish that you'll regret for the rest of your life."

"Maybe you're being a little too dramatic," Binky accused. "Lots of girls get pressured into sleeping with their boyfriends—even 'nice' ones. You and I both know that. There are lots of girls at school who have . . . well, you know."

"Oh, Binky . . ." Lexi was at a loss for words.

"Well, don't worry about it," Binky announced, jumping to her feet. "Harry's roommates aren't going away for a while yet. I guess I have some time to think about this."

"You shouldn't have to think about it. Just say, 'No, Harry.' "

"He said that if I loved him, I'd do it," Binky blurted.

"If he really loved you, he wouldn't ask you to do it."

"You're no help at all, Lexi." Binky moved toward the door. "And don't mention this to Egg. He'd disown me if he knew."

Before Lexi could say anything more, Binky was out the front door and down the steps. Lexi stared after her until Binky was out of sight.

"Oh, Father," she petitioned aloud. "Help! My friends need help, *big time*!"

Chapter Five

Lexi felt as though she were walking around in a deep, dark fog. The knowledge of Nancy's illness had changed everything. She was impatient with the lighthearted banter at school, and intolerant of the constant complaining her friends did about their homework and classes.

"I'm never going to make it through chemistry," Binky wailed as they left the lab. "This is the worst thing that's ever happened to me."

"It is not, Binky. Don't be silly. There are lots worse things that can happen than problems with a chemistry class."

Binky turned with a look of surprise at Lexi. "Sor-ry. I didn't know you'd be so touchy. I thought I could say how I felt around you . . ."

"Well, I'm not in the mood to hear complaining today, Binky. It just seems so . . . trivial."

"What *is* it with you, Lexi? You're so short-tempered—like a firecracker with a short fuse."

Lexi bit back another sharp retort. "Sorry."

"I thought maybe you and Todd had a fight," Binky mused. "But when I see you together, you talk like there's no one within a hundred miles, so I guess that's not it. I hope whatever's eating you blows over soon." Binky stamped off in a huff.

Lexi started to call after her friend but thought better of it. It was no use. As long as she felt this way, she'd just put her foot in her mouth again. Until she could get this thing with Nancy sorted out in her head, she felt unable to be a friend to anyone. All her thoughts and concerns were focused on Mike's fiancée in a hospital bed.

Maybe she should apologize to Binky for her and Todd's behavior. Lexi knew how difficult it had been for Todd to pretend things were normal. He was genuinely worried about his brother. Mike refused to come home from the hospital to do any more than shower and get a change of clothes.

He'd even turned the operation of the garage over to his employee, Ed Bell. He took paperwork to the hospital in a briefcase and worked on it while he sat by Nancy's bed.

Todd had become a messenger boy, running between Ed at the garage and Mike at the hospital.

"I'll apologize to Binky after health class," Lexi told herself. "I'll make her understand that my crankiness has nothing to do with her." Binky would forgive her. She would understand.

———

Lexi walked into health class and sat down. When she looked up at the chalkboard she gasped sharply. The posters and handwritten notes on the board conveyed a freaky coincidence.

"Today we're going to discuss the immune system," Mr. Drummond began. "I'm sure some of you have touched on this topic in biology class, but this is very important information, which bears repeating. For those of you who know it all already . . ."

A titter of suppressed giggles swept over the room.

". . . You can take some basic notes and get an A+ on the test. For those of you who aren't so sure of your materials, I'd recommend you pay close attention. In case you haven't discovered it yet, there's a reason why there's an emphasis on the immune system in both biology and health classes right now. The reason is the increased spread of Acquired Immune Deficiency Syndrome, or AIDS.

"AIDS is one of the most potent diseases to come along in your generation or mine."

"Haven't we heard enough about this?" Minda asked in a whiny voice from the back of the room. "We cover it in school, we hear about it at home, read about it in magazines, see it on television. Doesn't anyone give us credit for having any brains? Who would be stupid enough to put themselves in a position to contract AIDS?"

"A lot of talented, creative, wonderful people have died from AIDS, Minda. I doubt any of them were stupid, but many were uninformed, undereducated, or made some poor lifestyle choices. It's part of my duty as a teacher to try to prevent you from making the same mistake."

Minda shrank back in her chair. Mr. Drummond was usually an easygoing teacher. Today, determination was evident in his voice.

"AIDS destroys the T-cells in our bodies that fight off disease. When HIV, the virus that causes AIDS, attacks, it hits those healing cells and destroys them. The body has no other way to protect itself. Once the body is vulnerable, other diseases infect it. Viruses and bacteria invade, and finish off the destruction AIDS has begun. In a healthy person, viruses or bacteria might cause only a sniffle, a runny nose, or a cough; however, in an AIDS victim, that same virus or bacteria can develop into something as serious as a dangerous form of pneumonia."

Lexi heard Todd shift in the seat behind her. She gripped a pencil so tightly in her hand that it snapped.

"So you're saying that even though AIDS won't kill you, it wipes out your immune system so every other disease that's floating around in the atmosphere can take a shot at you," Tim Anders summarized, after Mr. Drummond acknowledged his raised hand.

Todd spoke up next. "You mean if you had AIDS, and then contracted pneumonia, you'd die?" Lexi could hear the tension in Todd's voice.

"Not necessarily. There are many antibiotics at our disposal to combat a particular illness. Unfortunately, even if an AIDS patient escapes one threat, there is always another one around the corner."

Lexi looked at the indifferent faces around her. It just wasn't real to them. It wouldn't hit home until someone they loved . . .

"Questions or comments anyone?" Mr. Drummond offered. "Tim, Brian?"

"Actually, this whole thing doesn't stir me up very much," Tim admitted. "I don't think AIDS is ever going to affect me, so I don't see why I should be worried about it."

Several others nodded in agreement.

"You mean you're *above* getting this illness?"

"Maybe not above it, but I'm not planning on doing any of the things people do to get AIDS," Tim said. A blush spread up his neck. "It's people who have sex with lots of partners or who do drugs that get it, right?"

"I have to agree with him, Mr. Drummond," Brian added hesitantly. "It's . . . other people . . . bad people . . . who get AIDS."

"What about people who get AIDS through blood transfusions—like hemophiliacs?" Egg suggested. "They aren't bad people, are they?"

"I think we should have more discussion about *how* people get AIDS," Minda said.

Tressa gave Minda a look of disgust. "I think anyone who gets AIDS was asking for it and probably deserves it. If you haven't done anything wrong, you won't get AIDS."

Before Mr. Drummond could contest Tressa's statement, Binky piped up. "It scares me. Do you think we should quit eating in restaurants? What if the plates and silverware aren't sterile, and you eat from a plate an AIDS victim has eaten from?"

"Or shake hands with someone who has AIDS," someone added.

"Ewww . . ." Binky shuddered, wiping her hands on her skirt. "I'm never shaking hands with anyone again."

"Class, class," Mr. Drummond raised his hand for order. "We will continue our discussion tomorrow. I think we all have different ideas about how the HIV virus is spread, and many of those assumptions are false."

Lexi turned to see how Todd was doing. He was pale and looked as though he might faint. Lexi was relieved when the class bell rang.

Todd bolted from his seat and out the door before Lexi could talk to him. She caught up with him in the hallway, where she found him leaning against the concrete wall, his eyes closed.

"Are you all right?"

"I guess so," he said dryly.

"I'll go home with you after school tonight."

"What about the Emerald Tones rehearsal?" he asked weakly.

"Your mom asked us to be at your house tonight, remember? The Emerald Tones will just have to get along without us."

"Maybe I should go to the Emerald Tones rehearsal, and you should go to my house," Todd said, attempting a weak joke. "I think it would be a whole lot easier to sing than to listen to my brother."

"Your mom says your family is the only support system Mike has right now. He needs you."

Todd looked into Lexi's eyes. "You're being terrific about this, you know. If I were you, I'd be tempted to run away from my family. We've got some pretty unsolvable problems."

"You're not going to get rid of me that easily," Lexi said. "I've been with you through a lot of good times. I'm not going to run away when things get rough."

———

It was after four-thirty when Todd and Lexi reached the Winston home. Mike's car was in the driveway, and Lexi could see him through the living room window, pacing back and forth. She followed Todd inside and stood by awkwardly as the two brothers embraced.

"How's it going?" Todd asked.

Mike had obviously been crying. He looked haggard and exhausted. "All the testing and retesting is done. The doctors are certain Nancy has AIDS." Mike drew a ragged breath and continued, "The good news is that the antibiotics are working. Nancy's going to make it—this time."

"That's great news, Mike."

"Is it?" Mike's expression was so bleak it made Lexi's heart ache. "What about next time? And the time after that? One of these days, some little bug is going to get ahold of her and not let go. I'm going to lose her, Todd."

"You've got to take this one day at a time, Mike."

"Yeah, right. One day at a time. It's pretty hard to stop looking ahead, though, when only a few weeks ago we were talking about spending the rest of our lives together."

"There have been some amazing breakthroughs in medical science," Todd offered weakly. "There are people working day and night looking for a cure. You can't give up hope."

Mike nodded. "I wish hope were something you could buy. I certainly need some right now."

"How is Nancy taking all this?" Lexi asked.

"Frankly, better than I am. She's strong, Lexi. Strong and positive."

"Will she keep her illness a secret?"

"Nancy hates secrets. There was a time in her life when she tried to keep things from her friends and family, but it didn't work out. It only hurt her. I don't believe she'll ever let that happen again."

Mike wiped away a tear. "I love her more than ever . . . Tonight she told me she was determined to face this thing head on. The hardest part is that she'll have to quit working with the babies that she loves so much." Tears flooded Mike's cheeks. "Nancy's had such a hard, hard life. She doesn't deserve to be hurt anymore."

Todd and Lexi sat down with Mike as he sank onto the couch. Mike's shoulders sagged, and he held his head in his hands. "I just don't know how we're going to get through this," he admitted brokenly. "Please continue to pray for us. We're going to need a lot of help."

After a long silence, Mike straightened his shoulders and lifted his head. "But we *will* get through. With God's help."

Chapter Six

"Are you ready for the youth meeting tonight?" Todd poked his head through the Leightons' open back door.

Lexi put the last dish into the dishwasher, latched the door, and turned it on. "Let me grab a jacket. I'll be right with you."

"What are you doing, Todd?" Ben came around the kitchen counter to greet his friend.

"We've got a meeting at church tonight. What are *you* doing?"

Ben held out a gray glob stuck to the palm of his hand. "I'm making stuff with clay. See?"

"Good for you. What are you going to make?"

"I've already made it!" Ben scolded. "It's a baseball."

"Oh, I should have known." Todd grinned and ruffled Ben's hair. "You keep yourself busy, don't you, little fella?"

"Sure do, big fella," Ben retorted. "Next, I'm going to make a pancake."

"Okay, I'm ready." Lexi emerged from the other room, slipping her arm into her jacket. "Bye, Ben. Be good."

"Bye, Lexi. You be good, too."

When they stepped outside, Lexi looked around, puzzled. "What? No car?"

"It needs work." Todd sighed. "You know what chaos there is at the shop. I'll be on foot for a month the way things are going."

"Maybe Ed could help you out with it some evening," Lexi suggested.

"The poor guy's doing all he can. He stays late and comes early. He's been busy outside the shop too. Ed signed up for a literacy tutor. He's learning to read."

"Hey, that's great!"

"He's excited about it. He brings flash cards to work and practices every chance he gets. I'm glad I had the opportunity to learn to read when I was a kid. It's something we all take for granted."

"We take a lot for granted, don't we?" Lexi answered.

"That's for sure," Todd said with a sad tone in his voice.

Egg, Binky, Peggy, and Jennifer were waiting at the corner when Todd and Lexi arrived. Lexi thought they all seemed rather subdued. Everyone was quiet as they walked toward the church.

Egg broke the ice. "So, what's new, Todd?" Then his face turned a ruddy color and he swallowed hard, his Adam's apple bobbing wildly.

"Not much." Todd stared at his friend. "Why are you acting so weird?"

"Nothing. Nothing. Ohmph!" Egg grunted as his sister jabbed him in the ribs with her elbow.

"Binky, what did you do that for?" Lexi asked.

They were behaving very oddly—even for Egg and Binky.

"Does anyone know what's happening at to-night's meeting?" Jennifer jumped into the conversation in an obvious attempt to divert attention from Egg and Binky's antics.

Lexi pretended not to notice. "It wasn't on the schedule Sunday. Sometimes Pastor Lake leaves it open, so he can slip a current topic into the meeting for discussion."

"I hope it's a round table night," Peggy said. "I like that format the best."

A round table at youth night usually meant a spirited discussion with Pastor Lake about a topic of his choice. This often resulted in some amazingly frank dialogue.

"You know what I like best about the round table?" Jennifer began. "The fact that Pastor Lake lets us ask any questions we want about a subject, and if we're too shy to ask we can write it out on paper."

"You? Too shy to ask a question? It's hard to imagine," Binky remarked.

"You never know. Some topics are pretty touchy."

"The really neat part is that it doesn't matter what your question is. Pastor Lake considers even the dumb ones seriously and really tries to answer them," Peggy said.

"I like the fact that everyone gets to join in," Binky said. "I've learned a lot from the round table talks."

"Do you know what I like the *least*?" Egg added. "When Minda and Tressa and some of the other Hi-Fives come to the meeting. They're always blurting out their bizarre opinions."

"But they create some interesting conversations, you must admit," Peggy said.

"Pretty interesting *arguments*, you mean," Jennifer countered.

"Even so, it's exciting," Peggy said. "You never know what will come up. Like the time Pastor Lake wanted to discuss teenage alcoholism—and I was struggling with just that problem."

"That was tense," Egg admitted.

"We've been through a lot together, haven't we?" Binky observed thoughtfully.

"We have." Todd put his arm around Binky's shoulders and gave her a squeeze. "I think we can get through just about anything together, don't you?"

Lexi knew exactly what Todd had in mind. Once word got out about Nancy's illness, there would be a multitude of questions from everyone they knew. The support and acceptance of friends was going to be very important to both Todd and Mike.

Anne Marie Arnold and Tim Anders were waiting in the doorway of the church. "Come on in. We're going to start in just a few minutes," Tim said.

When Egg and Todd went ahead, Binky grabbed Lexi by the wrist. "Come into the bathroom with me, Lexi," she whispered urgently.

"Aren't you coming?" Peggy said as she and Jennifer turned around to look at them.

Binky waved them on. "Save us a place." She pulled Lexi down the hallway to the rest room and practically shoved her inside.

"All right, what's going on?" Lexi demanded as Binky moved toward the mirror and began to fluff her hair.

"Do you have a comb?" Binky asked casually.

Lexi pulled a small one out of her purse. "Here. Binky, your hair looks fine. What is it that you wanted to talk to me about?"

Binky combed her hair, staring at Lexi in the mirror. "I just wanted to ask you if the rumors were true."

"What rumors?" Lexi knew that Cedar River High could be a real hotbed of information, not all of it true.

"You know. The *rumors*. I couldn't ask you in front of Todd, because of Mike and all."

"What do you mean, 'because of Mike and all'?" Lexi was beginning to feel nervous and hot.

"You know! The rumors about Nancy having a terrible disease?"

How could it be out already? Lexi thought, feeling sick to her stomach. *What am I going to say without betraying the Winstons' trust?* "A terrible disease?" Lexi answered cautiously, hoping Binky wouldn't press her.

"Well, I mean a disease that's caught in a . . . bad . . . way."

"Can a disease be caught in a 'good' way, Binky?" Lexi wondered if Binky could tell she was stalling. Nancy and Mike certainly hadn't had much time to deal with the diagnosis before the whole world learned their secret.

"I heard from somebody at school who knows somebody at the nursing home. That person had heard from someone at the hospital that there was a patient there with AIDS. The person at the hospital also said that the only patient in isolation right now was Mike's girlfriend, Nancy. That means she must be the person with AIDS. Right?"

"Oh, Binky . . ."

"You know perfectly well what I mean by a disease being caught in a bad way, Lexi. AIDS is a sexually transmitted disease. One you get when you have multiple sex partners, or do intravenous drugs with dirty needles."

"It sounds like you believe if someone has AIDS, they're a bad person, Binky."

Binky thought about it for a moment. "In a way, I guess I do."

"How can you say that?" Lexi was stunned. "All sex isn't bad, you know. Sex happens to be a beautiful part of marriage. Of course it is wrong and harmful outside of marriage."

"Oh, I'm not getting anywhere with you at all, Lexi! You're just trying to steer the subject away from Nancy." Binky paused. "Maybe you don't know anything about this after all. I was sure you would because you're so close to Todd." Binky fluffed her hair again. "Never mind. Forget what I said. It's probably not true anyway. I wish kids at school would quit gossiping. It would certainly be a lot easier on me."

Lexi trailed after Binky as she left the rest room, feeling hollow and empty inside. All her emotional energy was drained. She hadn't lied, but she hadn't told the truth either. The secret was not hers to tell. Binky had put her in a terrible spot.

Binky and Lexi were the last to join the youth group in the basement. It was obviously going to be a round table night. The room was full, and everyone had turned their chairs inward to make a circle. Pastor Lake sat near the door; next to him were Egg and Angela Hardy. Jennifer was sitting next to Matt Windsor. She'd saved two seats between her and Peggy.

"Come on, you guys! Where have you been?"

Lexi looked around the circle for Todd. His chair was directly opposite hers. He sat between Brian James and Tim Anders. They were in some sort of deep discussion.

Minda Hannaford and Tressa and Gina Williams had taken their usual spots near the kitchen. They always liked to be first in line for the snack. It was usually a comical race between the Hi-Fives and Egg and Binky to see who'd get to the food first.

"Welcome," Pastor Lake began. "It's good to see so many of you here tonight. I hope you came because you wanted to take part in a round table discussion." He smiled. It seemed to be his favorite format, too.

"What's the topic, Pastor Lake?" Tressa asked. "Something controversial, I hope."

"That's up to you and the rest of the group. I feel I've been taking too much control lately, by planning the programs, topics of discussion, and so on. Tonight the round table topic is up to you."

Everyone was quiet, apparently contemplating the freedom to choose a subject.

"Sometimes it's difficult to voice your questions and concerns," Pastor Lake said. "But I know you have them. To make it easier, why don't you each write down the biggest concern you have on your mind tonight. It may have to do with getting along with siblings, or friends. Maybe you argued with your parents before you came here. It really doesn't matter how trivial or how serious you feel your question is, just jot it down on a piece of paper, fold it in half, and hand it in." Pastor Lake began passing pieces of paper and pencils around the room. "We'll pick a question out of the pile and discuss it. We may have time for only one tonight, or we may have time for several."

Lexi closed her eyes and groaned inwardly. Pastor Lake couldn't have picked a worse night to do this. Her mind was reeling with many serious issues, none of which she felt she could talk about in public. Finally, because she saw everyone else turning their questions in, she scribbled something on her paper.

What do you do when people's lives are caving in around you? Lexi thought it was a crummy question, but she could hardly say, *What do you do when one friend has AIDS, and another wants to throw her virginity away?* Lexi folded the paper and passed it toward Pastor Lake. She wished she hadn't come tonight. After the incident with Binky in the bathroom, Lexi wasn't sure how long she could put off her friends' questions. She glanced across the circle to Todd. He looked pale and agitated.

"Has everyone turned in their questions?" Pastor Lake stuffed the papers into an offering basket, then began by reading several to himself. When he looked up, he had a bemused expression on his face. "There are several questions on the same theme," he commented. "To satisfy my own curiosity, I have to ask, what have you been studying in school lately?"

"French, chemistry, history," someone said.

"What about health class?" he asked. "What's been the most recent topic there?"

"AIDS," Tressa blurted. "It seems like every class we go to, we have to discuss it. It's getting old and boring, if you ask me."

"Ah-hah. That explains it," Pastor Lake said. "I would say probably half the questions here deal with the topic of AIDS. That's perfectly natural if you've been talking about it in school. There's no way that one class could cover everything you need or want to know about this disease. If it's okay with everyone, I think we should talk about it tonight."

Chapter Seven

Lexi could imagine what Todd must be thinking. He didn't need to hear this right now. Lexi didn't want to talk about it either, but there didn't seem to be any way out of it. Everyone, except perhaps Tressa Williams, seemed interested in discussing the topic again.

Pastor Lake took a deep breath. "Perhaps before we begin, we should define exactly what AIDS is for those who may still be uncertain about it."

"Here we go again," Tressa muttered.

"Doctors know now that people can carry HIV, or the Human Immunodeficiency Virus for as many as ten years before they actually get AIDS, or Acquired Immune Deficiency Syndrome, the disease that HIV causes," Pastor Lake began. "That's the scary thing about AIDS. Normal, healthy-looking people may be carrying the deadly virus. They can spread the disease before they even come down with it themselves."

"Why is it that we have only recently been hearing about it?" Brian James asked.

"The first case of AIDS was diagnosed in this country in 1981, but it has spread rapidly since then. And it will take many more lives before a cure is found."

"Do you mean to say that some of us here could have AIDS and not even know it?" Binky asked. "That's creepy."

"It's possible, Binky," Pastor Lake said. "But even if there were a person who was HIV positive on either side of you, you couldn't get the disease by sitting next to him, or even by touching him."

At that moment, Egg raised his head. "Ah . . . ah . . . ah . . . choo!" The explosive sneeze startled everyone in the room and made Binky cringe.

"Ewwww! Gross, Egg!" she howled.

Pastor Lake smiled. "You can't get AIDS from someone sneezing on you either."

"I'm scared." Binky's eyes grew big and round. Lexi could tell she wasn't being overly dramatic, either. Binky looked genuinely frightened.

"The virus isn't so strong that it can swim rivers and climb mountains to get to you," Pastor Lake assured her. "You have to be engaged in dangerous practices in order to become infected. You're not going to get it from sitting on a toilet seat or shaking hands. The AIDS virus can't pass through skin that isn't broken or cut. AIDS has to enter your bloodstream. You don't have to be afraid to grasp a doorknob or use a telephone that's been touched by someone who has the virus. And the AIDS virus dies when it comes in contact with air."

"What if someone was really sweaty and put his arm around you, or you ate something from the plate of a person with the AIDS virus?" Egg asked.

"I don't believe they've found the AIDS virus to exist in human perspiration. Many families who care for AIDS patients use the same plates and silverware. Sharing food and utensils is not a problem."

"It would be for me," Binky muttered.

Lexi could almost see the self-protective wall Binky was building around herself. Even talking about the disease frightened her, so that she withdrew from the people around her. Oddly enough, Lexi was almost sure Binky still didn't connect this with what she was considering with Harry.

"Is AIDS really all that bad?" someone near Lexi asked. "Everyone always talks like it's a death sentence or something."

Pastor Lake's expression was grim. "It *is* a death sentence. AIDS is a fatal disease."

"You mean no one ever survives it?"

"Anyone with AIDS will eventually die as a result of it, because they will not be able to resist other diseases."

There was a heavy silence in the room.

"What are we going to do about it? Shouldn't they test everybody for AIDS and then put the people who have it somewhere?"

"And where would you propose they put all these people, Binky?"

"I don't know. Somewhere away from the rest of us. I mean, really, should they be walking on the streets when they could infect healthy people?"

"Binky, don't be such a dope," Jennifer said. "We aren't going to get AIDS. We're all healthy, and we are not going to do stupid things. It's something that happens to other people. I doubt if there's a person here in Cedar River who has AIDS, so I wouldn't worry about it."

Pastor Lake listened thoughtfully to the exchange. "I believe the truth is somewhere between your two statements. The world is not going to disappear over night if we don't take all the people with AIDS and banish them to some distant land. On the other hand, indifference is not the answer either. We can't count on medicine, science, and good luck to take care of everything. It's important that you be informed. You can only protect yourself against an enemy if you know all there is to know about it. Don't be complacent. The AIDS virus is not limited by age, sex, or skin color."

"But can't we do something about it?" Binky pleaded.

"It is preventable, Binky. It doesn't float in the air and strike randomly. We have the ability to make moral, God-directed choices about our bodies."

"I sure want to prevent it!" Tim blurted.

"The basics to insure personal health and safety are to abstain from sex before marriage, and to say no to drugs. The only really safe sex outside of marriage is *no sex*. You are in charge of your body. You can make the choices that will keep it healthy."

"I don't think we should discuss this anymore," Tressa said wearily. "I'm sick and tired of it. My dad says people who get AIDS deserve it."

Lexi looked at Todd. She knew the willpower he must be exercising to remain silent.

"How can anyone deserve something as awful as AIDS?" Anna Marie asked.

"Well, if they weren't having sex with a bunch of partners or doing drugs, they wouldn't get it. A person who does those things is asking for trouble," Tressa answered.

"But what about children who contract AIDS from their mothers at birth, or hemophiliacs who have gotten the virus through blood transfusions?" Pastor Lake asked.

Tressa shrugged, unsure how to answer that one.

"Maybe there are good ways to get AIDS," Binky suggested. "When little kids and hemophiliacs get AIDS, they haven't done anything wrong."

"I agree with Binky," Jennifer said. "Some people can't help it if they get AIDS. Others can."

"If I were going to get it, I'd want to get it through a transfusion," Egg said. "It wouldn't be nearly so embarrassing."

"Transfusions are much safer now because blood is tested before it's used," Pastor Lake said. "But if you did get it through surgery or a transfusion, you would still die."

Pastor Lake appeared disturbed by the turn the discussion had taken. "Listen to yourselves and think about what you're saying!" he said.

"Pastor Lake," Minda began, "you'd never approve of my doing drugs. But if I were in an accident and had a blood transfusion and contracted AIDS, you wouldn't blame me for being sick."

"I don't blame anyone for being sick," Pastor Lake said evenly. "But I am a little stunned at your narrow-mindedness."

"Can't we have our own opinions?"

"Of course. But the opinion that there are good and bad ways of contracting the disease is a false division. It's all the same disease. AIDS victims should be treated with love and compassion, not as dirty or sinful. We have this problem in the church today. Every time we talk about AIDS, we get bogged down discussing the morality of the disease, when we should be thinking of ways the church can help to meet its challenges, such as encouraging education and abstinence for the healthy, and compassion and care for the sick."

"I agree with Pastor Lake," Todd announced.

He'd been quiet so long, Lexi was sure Todd wasn't going to say anything.

But he continued. "AIDS victims are sick. They're hurting. They don't need anybody kicking them while they're down, pointing fingers in their faces, saying they're sinful. And they sure don't need to see certain people treated with compassion, because they got the disease in an innocent way."

"But Todd, it still stands that people who get AIDS by sharing drug needles or having unprotected sex know better and are asking for it," Tressa insisted.

"Not everyone knows . . ."

"Well, if they don't, they should. Teachers hammer it into us constantly. I think AIDS is God's way of punishing people for bad living. It's so clear, I can't believe people don't get it," Tressa said disgustedly.

"I don't see how anyone can agree with that, Tressa," Todd countered. "The God I believe in is loving and forgiving. I don't think He punishes people by giving them AIDS. I wouldn't want to believe in a God like that."

"Todd is right in the sense that AIDS is not a punishment. It is a matter of cause and effect. We live in a fallen world," Pastor Lake explained.

He allowed the debate to continue as the young people stated their opinions on either side of the issue. Some agreed with Tressa, and others supported Todd's view. It was frightening for Lexi to see how agitated and angry some of her friends and peers became over the subject.

Pastor Lake finally broke into the argument. "You are not the first group, nor will you be the last, to debate this issue."

"You mean there are other people who aren't smart enough to see the real picture?" Tressa said, crossing her arms over her chest. Minda and Gina followed suit, mimicking her hostile stance.

"AIDS isn't about good and bad people, Tressa," Pastor Lake said. "AIDS is about pain and suffering. And who is better able to help those who suffer than the church?"

"But—"

"The HIV virus that causes AIDS isn't prejudiced. It grows wherever it is allowed to enter—in a homosexual victim or a heterosexual one. Eventually, it kills them all."

"We Christians have to stop blaming and judging. It's time to start loving and helping those in trouble."

"That's pretty hard sometimes," Binky said quietly. "It would be scary taking care of an AIDS patient."

"When I am struggling with an issue," Pastor Lake said, "as I see some of you doing tonight, I ask myself the question: 'If Jesus were here, what would He do?' "

Lexi was stunned by the simplicity of Pastor Lake's question.

"If Jesus were on earth today, to whom would He minister?"

"Poor people," someone suggested.

"Sick people," another responded.

"AIDS victims," Lexi stated firmly.

"Then if that is the case, how can we do any less?"

Pastor Lake glanced around the room. "I think it would be a good idea to take a break now and have our snack. I know you have more questions, some of which have no concrete answers. But if you'd like to continue discussion of the subject, we can do so."

Many began to stand and move toward the kitchen. Lexi heard Tressa say to Minda, "I don't know what more there is to discuss; I know I'm right."

Todd moved against the flow of people toward the outside door. Lexi followed him and found him outside, leaning against a brick wall.

"Are you all right, Todd?"

He didn't open his eyes. A tear slid from under one eyelid. "I'll never be convinced that Nancy deserved this. *Never*. No matter what Tressa or anyone says, no one deserves this disease. If Christians think that, I don't want to have anything to do with them."

Without saying anything, Lexi took Todd's hand and held it firmly in hers. She was frightened. This incident in Todd's family was much more complicated than she had ever dreamed possible.

Chapter Eight

"Can I walk home with you, Lexi?" Binky asked as she shoved books into her locker after school.

"Sure. Is Egg coming too?"

"No. He's got work to do on the *Cedar River Review*. Are you sure Todd won't mind if you don't ride with him?"

"He wasn't in school today."

"Oh, yeah, I forgot."

Binky *had* been distracted. She'd also been unusually subdued. Harry Cramer certainly hadn't done Binky any favors by forcing her to make a decision about having sex to keep their dating relationship.

"Let's go. I promised Ben I'd play with him after school today." Lexi started out and Binky trailed after her. It wasn't until they were nearly halfway home that Binky spoke.

"Harry called." Lexi could hear the nervous tremor in her voice. "He asked me again to come and stay with him in the dorm."

"What did you say?" Lexi struggled to sound nonchalant. If Binky realized how much this upset Lexi, she might not confide in her.

"What *could* I say? Harry was so excited that he did most of the talking. He got an A + on a math test and said he had a pretty good chance on a good grade in history . . ."

"What did he say about the two of you?"

"Just that his roommates were going away for a weekend soon. He really wants me to come, Lexi."

"Of course he does. But I think he's being totally selfish. He's asking you to do things you don't want to do."

"I don't know *what* I want anymore!" Binky wailed.

"He never should have put you in a position like this!" Lexi said sternly.

"It's not so easy for him, you know." Binky came to her boyfriend's defense. He's under a lot of pressure, too."

"What kind of pressure?"

"Harry's roommates are—sexually active," Binky blurted. "He told me so. He said they spend weekends with their girlfriends all the time."

"That doesn't make it smart or right for you," Lexi pointed out.

"But they've been giving him a really hard time about being a virgin. They tell him that it's time he grew up and had some experience with girls."

"I've never even met Harry's roommates, and I don't think I like them," Lexi commented. "They sound horrible."

"I think Harry wants to find out what he's missing, that's all. You can understand that."

"He's not missing anything that he's supposed to have right now, Binky. Sex is for married people. His roommates are the ones in the wrong."

"I guess Harry told them that, and they called him a goody-two-shoes and made fun of him. Besides, it made Harry ask himself, 'Why *do* teenagers have to wait until they get married to have sex?' "

"Because the Bible says, 'Run away from sexual sin . . . The one who sins sexually, sins against his own body.' God wants to protect us from doing things that will harm us. If you sin with your body, Binky, it hurts your soul. Having casual sex with a guy before marriage sounds like sexual sin to me, and it has a lot of scary, long-term consequences."

"But Harry's my boyfriend! I might even marry him someday."

"Do you love him?"

"I'm not sure . . ."

"Well, then you probably aren't going to marry him. Anyway, my mom says that sex between a married couple is a hundred times better, because there's no guilt, no fear of disease, and you're completely committed to each other. In the long run, Binky, having sex with Harry now can only hurt you."

"I just can't see how it would hurt me that much!"

"You could get pregnant, for starters."

"There are ways to prevent that."

"You could get AIDS or another sexually transmitted disease."

"Lexi, I wouldn't be having sex with anyone but Harry. So how could I get any of that stuff?"

"How do you know Harry hasn't slept with someone else?"

"Well, I doubt that very much."

"But you don't know for sure. Besides, you could ruin your own self-respect. You aren't cheap, Binky. Don't give yourself away. Especially not to a guy who just wants to satisfy his curiosity! Save yourself for your husband. It makes a great wedding present."

"I wish this had never come up between Harry and me!" Binky said dejectedly. "I'm too young to have to make all these decisions."

"That's exactly my point," Lexi said.

"I'll have to think about it some more," Binky said as she turned up the sidewalk to her house. "See you later. And—thanks for listening."

"Right. See you later." Lexi sighed deeply, then continued walking slowly toward her house, mulling over in her mind the conversation with Binky. It wasn't only bad kids who faced the issue of premarital sex, but good ones—people like Binky McNaughton, who was one of the dearest, sweetest friends Lexi had. It was becoming apparent to her that there weren't any easy answers about issues like this.

———

"Don't move your man there, Ben. Otherwise I'm going to take all your checkers," Lexi warned.

Ben studied the red-and-black board intently. "I'm not a baby, Lexi. You don't have to tell me what to do. I wanna move it here." Ben pushed his checker piece into the spot he'd had his eye on.

"You'll be sorry, Benjamin."

"I know how to play, Lexi. I can decide."

Lexi sighed and made a big production of jumping four of Ben's men, wiping him off the playing board.

"Oh no!" Ben put his hands to his forehead and rocked back and forth. "You did it, Lexi."

"I told you I would."

"Let's play again."

"Maybe later, Ben, when your luck changes," Lexi said with a chuckle. "Right now I think I'll go to Todd's house."

"You haven't seen me all day, Lexi. I've been in school."

"I know, Ben, but I haven't seen Todd either," Lexi explained. "He wasn't in school today."

"Is he sick?"

"I don't think so," Lexi reassured her little brother. "He just has a lot of things on his mind."

"What does that mean?"

"Todd's family has had some problems lately, and he's been worrying about them."

"Worry gives you a tummyache," Ben said knowingly. "Poor Todd." Ben got up, walked around the table, and pulled on Lexi's arm until she stood up. "You'd better go see Todd right away."

Lexi leaned over and hugged her brother. "Thanks, sweetheart. I'll play another game of checkers with you later."

Lexi thought about the whole situation again as she walked toward the Winston home. Todd had been unusually upset the last time she talked to him. It had been a tough week for the whole family, but especially for Mike. Fortunately, Nancy had rallied and was released from the hospital yesterday. The family was taking it one day at a time—the way people should always live their lives, Lexi thought. *It's too bad people can't learn to enjoy one day at a time without having to face a tragedy like this first.*

Mike's car was parked in the driveway. Lexi rang the doorbell and was surprised when Ed, from the garage, opened the door.

"Ed! I didn't expect to see you here."

"Come on in. Mike asked me to come over."

"You're both here? What about the garage?"

"I just locked it up for a while. I hung an Out-to-

Lunch sign on the door. Nothing wrong with that, is there?" His cheerful, lopsided grin made Lexi feel better immediately.

Ed was long and lanky like Egg. He was also good-natured and comfortable to be around.

"What's new with you today?" Ed asked Lexi, making no move to lead her into the living room.

"Todd wasn't in school. I thought I'd stop over and see how he's doing. It's been pretty grim around here, hasn't it?"

Ed rolled his eyes and tilted his head toward the living room. "You'd better come in and see who's here."

Lexi followed Ed into the living room and was surprised to see Mike and Nancy sitting together on the couch. Nancy was much paler and thinner, but her eyes lit up with pleasure when she saw Lexi.

"Hi, Lexi. How are you?"

"Nancy, it's so good to see you out of the hospital!"

Nancy patted the couch beside her. "Come, sit down. Tell me about school."

A thought broke into Lexi's mind. *If I sit next to her, I might have to touch her. . . .* But Pastor Lake's words followed close behind: *You can't get the AIDS virus by sitting next to someone who has it.*

Lexi moved toward Nancy, ashamed of the fear she'd felt. If she could be afraid when she *wanted* to be close to Nancy, it was no wonder people who didn't understand the disease were afraid!

She dropped down onto the couch and reached for Nancy's hand. "You look great. A little thinner, maybe."

"Hospital food. It's terrible. I'm ashamed, but as

a nurse I fed that stuff to poor, unsuspecting patients for years."

"The food didn't look so bad to me," Mike protested, struggling to be cheerful and upbeat.

"Mike, you could eat shoe leather if you put salt and pepper on it," Nancy pointed out. "I hardly picture you as a connoisseur of fine dining."

"Of course not. If I can't spell it or pronounce it, how could I *be* it?"

"By the way, Lexi, thanks for the sweet teddy bear you and Todd brought to the hospital. I'm sorry I didn't get to see you. I must have been feeling pretty ragged then."

"Oh, hi, Lexi, I didn't know you were here." Todd walked into the room with a tray of sandwiches.

"Ed let me in."

"Then it looks like we're having a party." Todd set the sandwiches on the table. "I'll go get the chips and sodas and we're all set."

"Where are your folks?" Lexi asked.

"Mom had a dinner meeting and she wanted Dad to go along. They thought they'd be home between nine and ten. Mike took Nancy for a drive and they ended up here."

As they ate and talked, Lexi felt awkward somehow. The conversation seemed to dance around the issue of Nancy's illness, never actually touching on it. It was frustrating to engage in small talk when there were so many important issues to discuss. It wasn't until Todd had passed out ice cream bars that Nancy took it upon herself to say what the others had been avoiding.

"I know this is very uncomfortable for you, Lexi, and you too, Ed. We're all sitting here, trying to pretend that nothing is wrong. We're acting cheerful and perfectly happy, like nothing's changed. You don't have to pretend any longer, at least not around me." She looked from Ed to Lexi and back again. "You know the disease that I have, of course."

Ed's shoulders slumped, and he nodded sadly. "Mike told me. I didn't want to believe it."

"Me, either," Lexi added. "It doesn't seem possible, Nancy. Not you. I'm so sorry."

"It's okay, Lexi. I'm sorry, too," Nancy admitted. "If there were any way to change it, I would. But no matter what I do, I'm still going to have AIDS. I've decided that the best way to deal with it is to be straightforward and honest."

"I thought you wouldn't want to talk about it," Lexi said.

Nancy looked at Mike with an expression of love and trust that wrenched Lexi's heart. "Mike and I have decided the best thing for us to do is to be open about my illness."

"You wouldn't have to, you know, Nancy," Ed said. "I'm sure there are others with the disease who just don't say anything . . ."

"I know, but that would catch up with me sooner or later, Ed. Lies always do. Besides, I might not have a very long life, and I don't want to live a lie. I hate deceit and pretense. There's nothing about my life that I *want* to hide." Nancy looked at Mike again, and Lexi could see the pain in her eyes.

"I've had to learn the hard way," Nancy began. "I've mentioned this to Todd and Lexi before . . ." She smiled at the confusion Ed's expression showed. "There was a time in my life I am very ashamed of now. The choices I made then have resulted in the disease I have today. I wish I'd learned early to live my life in a manner that left no regrets. Unfortunately, that was not the case."

"We're your friends, Nancy," Lexi said. "It doesn't matter what you tell us. We'll still be your friends."

Tears welled up in Nancy's eyes. "You don't know how good it feels to hear you say that, Lexi. I do need to talk about how I used to be. It helps me sort things out, and it might help someone else."

"Nancy, you don't have to . . ." Ed began.

"I know, but I want to. I don't want anyone else to make the same mistakes I did. If someone had warned me about having premarital sex back then, I probably would have laughed in his face," Nancy said bluntly. "Even 'safe sex' is a silly-sounding phrase. Who would have dreamed ten years ago that having sex could lead to a fatal disease?"

Mike winced at Nancy's words but said nothing. Obviously he and Nancy had already talked about what she was telling the others.

"But ten years ago I was sixteen and already sexually active. The last thing I had on my mind in the heat of passion was catching some disease. If I *had* thought of it, I might have avoided what I have to face now."

Ed coughed uncomfortably. "You don't look like the type . . ."

"To be promiscuous?" Nancy asked. "It's something you can't tell about a person just by looking at them. I was a rebel with low self-esteem. That's a bad combination.

"Even after I first heard about AIDS, I didn't worry. After all, it seemed that at that time the only people who were in any danger were homosexuals. I thought nothing could touch me. If anyone had tried to convince me that the only safe sex was no sex at all, I would not have believed them.

"I made one bad decision after the other. My first was to have sex outside of marriage. That is something I desperately wish I had saved for my husband-to-be." Nancy took Mike's hand in hers. "What made that bad decison even worse was that once I decided to have sex, I didn't protect myself." Nancy looked directly at Lexi, and it made her blush.

"Nancy, do you think all this needs to be said to Todd and Lexi?" Mike asked.

"Yes, I do, Mike. This is a life or death issue we're talking about. That's what young people don't realize. The decisions they make in the heat of the moment can determine whether or not they're going to live or die. I know now that having sex outside of marriage is wrong, stupid, and harmful. Back then, I didn't want to hear what God had to say about it."

Nancy looked at Ed. "It's like I said, you can't tell by looking at a person whether or not he or she has had several sex partners or is carrying a disease. The doctors believe that I've been carrying the AIDS virus for at least eight years. It's taken that long for it to show up."

Tears flooded Nancy's eyes. "It's ironic, isn't it? I spent three years of my life being wild and reckless before I accepted Christ as my Savior. Now, just before I'm to marry the first and only man I've ever really loved, this disease rears its ugly head and threatens to kill me." Nancy shuddered. "It terrifies me to think about it. I put my life in danger over and over again and called it 'having fun.'"

Nancy gave Mike a loving glance. "The most wonderful gift is Mike's forgiveness and acceptance. I hope all of you can forgive me, too. I'm sorry if I've disappointed you."

Lexi gave Nancy a hug. She felt so frail, but Lexi squeezed her tightly. "Nancy, I love you even more now. You're so brave. It can't be easy to talk about your past or admit your mistakes, especially when you have to cope with this horrible disease."

"Do you mean that, Lexi, that you still love me?" For the first time, Nancy's voice wavered.

"Of course she does, and I do, too," Todd said firmly. "We don't love you any less now than we did before. We know God has forgiven you for your past, and we do, too."

Ed reached out for Nancy's hand. "What are friends for, anyway? I was afraid people would look down on me when they discovered I couldn't read or write. I hid my secret so long it became like a festering sore that made me sick inside. Once I opened up and admitted that I couldn't read, instead of laughing at me, you supported me and helped me. You gave me back my self-esteem. Friends don't give up on friends just because they aren't perfect. They do all they can for them. We'd like to do that for you, Nancy."

There were tears streaming down Nancy's cheeks as she turned to Mike. "Oh, Mike. You were right."

"I told you." Mike brushed a lock of hair from Nancy's forehead. "I knew none of them would let you down."

Lexi looked at Mike and Nancy with mixed emotions—joy and apprehension. Their love was so beautiful, but so temporary. How long would Nancy live?

Chapter Nine

The doorbell rang sharply. Ed jumped to answer it.

"Hi, Egg. Hi, Binky." Ed's voice carried into the living room.

"Is Lexi here?" Binky asked. "We stopped at her house. Ben said she'd walked over here."

"She's here. Come in." Ed ushered the pair toward the living room. They stood on the threshold like a pair of deer frozen in the headlights of a car, staring at Nancy and Mike as they sat on the couch. Whatever else they had expected, Lexi decided, they did not expect to find Nancy here.

Lexi remembered her encounter with Binky in the rest room of the church. Now she could almost see the wheels spinning in Binky's head as her friend put two and two together. Binky had heard the rumor of Nancy's illness, and now she was confronting her face-to-face. Lexi could sense her friend's dismay and confusion.

"Uh . . . hi," Binky blurted. "We didn't realize we were interrupting something. We can go and come back another time. Come on, Egg." Binky grabbed her brother's hand and tried to turn away.

Ed put his hands on their shoulders and pushed

them into the room. "This isn't a meeting. We're celebrating Nancy's release from the hospital."

"We're glad you're out, Nancy. Are you feeling better?" Egg said politely. Lexi noticed he didn't advance any farther.

"Much better, thanks."

"We missed you at school today, Todd," Binky said.

"It was boring, as usual," Egg added.

"Would you like to sit down?" Todd offered.

Egg and Binky exchanged a glance and shook their heads in unison. "No, we have to go," Egg said. "We just wanted to know if you were all right, Todd."

Their discomfort was achingly apparent. Neither wanted to be rude, nor did they want to come any closer to Nancy. They appeared paralyzed with indecision.

"Thanks for the beautiful card you sent when I was in the hospital," Nancy said. "Ed, show them that basket of cards and stuff."

Ed picked up a wicker basket full of cards and small gifts. "Would you like to look at them?"

Binky reached for them and then drew back as if there were spiders in the basket instead of cards. "Maybe another time," Binky stammered. "Come on, Egg, I think we'd better go. *Now.*"

They stumbled over each other in their race for the front door and were gone.

Todd was the first to speak. "I'm sorry, Nancy. They must have heard . . . I mean, the rumor must be out . . ."

"That's not like Egg and Binky," Lexi murmured.

Mike looked hurt. "They didn't want to get near you."

"I wouldn't have asked them in if I'd known it was going to be so awkward," Ed said.

"It's okay. But please don't apologize to me," Nancy said. "I may be ill, but there's nothing wrong with my hearing or my eyesight. I know exactly what was wrong with Egg and Binky. They were afraid."

Mike shook his head, anguish showing in his face.

"I have AIDS. They don't understand what that means for them, for their safety. That's why they didn't want to come near me or touch my things. I can't say that I blame them."

Nancy folded her hands and leaned back on the couch with a smile. She actually looked happier than she had all afternoon.

"You aren't even upset, are you?" Todd observed.

Nancy didn't look the least bit upset, only excited and determined. "Egg and Binky just did me a marvelous favor," she announced.

Everyone stared at her, puzzled.

"A favor?" Mike asked. "What kind of a favor?"

"They helped me to make up my mind. Ever since the doctors gave me their diagnosis, I've been wondering how to make my past mistakes work for good in someone else's life. Egg and Binky just showed me how."

"All Egg and Binky showed us was how to be jerks," Todd said tartly.

"Todd! Don't be like that," Nancy scolded. "Their visit was exactly what I needed. Now I know what I'm going to do with the rest of my life. Because I'm a nurse, I already understand the human body, the immune system, and how viruses work. I've taken care of AIDS victims. Now I *am* one.

"Because of my training and my experience, I can

educate others. Education is one way to stop the virus from spreading. We can help change attitudes like Binky's and Egg's through education. The McNaughtons are two of the greatest young people I've ever met. They're just confused and frightened. They don't know how to act around an AIDS victim. Education can change that.

"Of course that doesn't mean education is the *only* answer. Whether or not to have premarital sex or do drugs is a moral decision each person has to make for himself. You either know it's wrong or you don't. But I can't go into every home and raise every child according to God's plan. What I *can* do is educate— and the sooner the better."

"Settle down, Nancy," Mike urged.

"I'm in too much of a hurry to settle down. Don't you see, Mike? I have so many things to accomplish while I still feel well."

"Nancy, you can't take on the whole world. You can't change everything."

"No, but I can try to make a difference." Nancy took Mike's hands and held them to her cheeks. "It's wonderful, Mike. God's given me a new purpose for my life."

"Just how do you plan to manage this?" Mike's tone was doubtful.

She smiled a bright, joyous smile. "You'll just have to wait and see."

———

Lexi met Mr. and Mrs. Winston in the hallway as she was leaving. It struck her that everyone had been paying so much attention to Mike and Nancy that no one had thought much about Mike's parents.

"Going home already?" Mrs. Winston seemed surprised. "It sounds as if the party is still in full swing."

"I promised Ben a game of checkers. He's probably waiting at the kitchen table with the board all set."

"He is such a sweetie." Mrs. Winston gave Lexi an affectionate smile. "Your parents have lovely children, Lexi."

"So do you."

Mrs. Winston's eyes glistened with tears. "And I thank God for them every day."

Impulsively, Lexi reached out to embrace Todd's mother. "I'm sorry your family is having so much trouble," she blurted.

"Thank you for your compassion, Lexi." Mrs. Winston appeared so tranquil and composed.

"It must be hard for you, Mrs. Winston," Lexi said sincerely. "If I had a son who was engaged to a person who has AIDS, I don't know if I could be as gracious."

Mrs. Winston smiled gently. "It's not easy, Lexi. Sometimes I want to cry and scream, 'Why Mike? Why Nancy?' It would be easy to be angry with Nancy for bringing this into our family, but I know that would not be the correct response."

"Pastor Lake told us at youth group the other night that people who are sick, especially with something as serious as AIDS, need all the love and compassion we can give them."

"That is so true. And we must remember that all of us have sinned. It's just that some sins have outward consequences that are visible to everyone. God loves us even though we have sinned, and He wants to forgive us. That makes Nancy and me more alike than we are different. I will never turn her away. She needs me now more than ever."

Chapter Ten

"Hey, Lexi, where's Todd?" Matt Windsor spoke from across the hallway.

Lexi removed her jacket and hung it in her locker. "I don't know. Maybe he isn't here yet. It's still early."

"Not that early." Minda Hannaford sauntered toward them. "I saw Todd a couple of minutes ago, but he looked like he was in a hurry. I really wanted his opinion on whether I should cover the biker look in my fashion column."

"Do you think Todd really cares?" Matt gave Minda an incredulous look.

She sniffed and stuck her chin out. "Matt, you are so behind the times. Fashion is the pulse of our culture. Haven't you read that hemlines go up and down with the state of the economy?"

"That's the stupidest thing I've ever heard!" Jennifer Golden joined them. "Minda, there are people starving in this country. How can you say it matters whether your skirt is long or short?"

"You people just have no sense of taste," Minda retorted. "I'll have to find someone who understands these things. Tressa, Gina, wait up." Minda dashed off, leaving Matt laughing, and Jennifer and Lexi shaking their heads.

"Only Minda can create a crisis out of a hem length," Jennifer muttered.

"Sorry I can't join you in this conversation," Matt said with a sheepish grin, "but if you see Todd, tell him I want to talk to him before class."

After Matt had gone, Jennifer turned to Lexi. "Can you believe Minda? Even when she's trying to be *nice* she drives me nuts. She can be so shallow sometimes."

Lexi had to agree. Even though she loved clothes and spent some of her free time sketching and designing them, lately it hadn't seemed important to her. Knowing what Todd's family was going through right now had made her stop to reevaluate her priorities.

"What are you thinking about?" Jennifer asked. "You look so grim."

"Just putting a few things into perspective," Lexi admitted. Before she could say more, Egg and Binky came up with Tim Anders in tow.

"What did you guys do this weekend?" Jennifer asked.

"Nothing much," Tim said. "I went over to Matt's, and we worked on his motorcycle on Saturday. That dumb machine is in parts and pieces on the garage floor more than it's together. Matt had planned to take it over to Mike Winston's garage," Tim continued, "but it was closed."

"Did any of you go to the Hi-Fives' party?" she asked.

"I didn't know they had one," Egg answered. "Not that I would have gone, even if I *had* been invited. Angela and I went miniature golfing." He took a practice golf swing, whooshing his arms through the air. "We were pretty good too, if I do say so myself. Parred five holes."

"You'll be going on the pro circuit pretty soon, Egg," Lexi told him.

"Think I could earn enough to make a living playing miniature golf?" Egg swung again. "I'd go for it if I could. Then I wouldn't have to take any more English classes."

"You'd still have to speak English, Egg, even as a professional," Binky reminded him.

"All that reading could be dangerous." Egg rolled his eyes. "My brain can't take it. I really shouldn't be stuffing anything more into it."

"That's been your problem for years, Egg," Binky said, "an overstuffed brain."

"Thanks, sis. It takes one to know one."

"What are you trying to tell me, Egg McNaughton?"

"I can't tell you anything. You never listen to me anyway . . ."

Egg and Binky were off and running, fueling their ongoing feud. Lexi listened to the conversations buzzing around her. It all sounded so . . . normal. Until now, she had taken "normal" for granted. Ever since she'd learned of Nancy's illness, Lexi had the feeling nothing would ever be normal again—for her, or for the Winston family.

"Lexi, could I talk to you for a minute?" Egg and Jennifer had drifted off, leaving Binky behind.

"Sure. What's up?"

"I just wanted you to know that I talked to Harry this weekend."

"Oh?" Lexi stopped walking and stood still in the middle of the hallway.

"I told him I wouldn't be staying the weekend with him."

Lexi sighed with relief. "Oh, I'm so glad!"

"I told him it was a dumb idea to satisfy his curiosity by getting involved in something that could hurt us both for the rest of our lives. I also told him I was going to wait until I got married to have sex, and that I considered it the best wedding gift I could give my husband. I told him that the man I loved wasn't going to get used, secondhand goods. Besides that, I told him that in this day of AIDS awareness, he was even dumber than I thought if he went out looking for sex."

Lexi had to laugh to herself at how Binky quoted almost exactly what Lexi had told her. *I guess it paid off to tell her up front what I thought.*

"Way to go, Binky! You did exactly the right thing."

"I know." The grin that spread across Binky's face told how proud she was.

"What did Harry have to say about your decision?"

"That's the really crazy part. He was *relieved*!"

"What? After putting you through all this?"

"Yes. I've never heard anyone sound so happy to be turned down. He admitted that his roommates had really been hassling him, but that he actually didn't feel ready himself for—you know what. Now he can tell them that I said 'no way,' and that he respects me too much to pressure me anymore. Besides that, Harry told me that the man I married was going to be the luckiest man on earth! He said that he hoped that whoever *he* married would save herself for him!"

"Men!" Lexi exclaimed. "They've got to be the most confusing creatures on earth!"

"Can you believe it, Lexi? He was caving in to peer pressure, and it wasn't even something he wanted or was ready for! What if I'd said yes?" Binky shuddered at the thought. "I would have thrown myself away for the most stupid reason imaginable!"

"Too many girls do, Binky. And I'm sure plenty of them regret it later. Usually they aren't as lucky as you. Their boyfriends pressure them in the backseat of a car instead of over the telephone. At least you had a chance to think clearly about what Harry was asking you to do."

"I did more than think," Binky corrected. "I *prayed*. Like I have never prayed in my life. And the neat thing about it is that I got an answer! It was so clear in my mind that it was like God spoke to me out loud. He told me to wait, because He's got better plans for me." Her face beamed. "It was great, Lexi! It was like God and I were having a conversation. I know you talk to God like that, but until this weekend I didn't realize I could, too."

"He always answers. It's just that sometimes we're not listening."

"Well, I know now that before I make any big decisions, I'm going to ask Him about it first." The class warning bell rang and Binky tore down the hall. "Gotta go, Lex."

Life as a Christian is just too amazing, Lexi mused. *What a totally awesome God we have.*

Lexi still hadn't moved, her thoughts turning to Nancy and her awful illness, when Peggy pulled on Lexi's sleeve. "What are you standing here for? You'll be late for class."

Lexi and Peggy walked into the classroom as the last bell rang. It wasn't until Lexi found her seat that she realized Todd wasn't in class. Had something happened to Nancy? Lexi bit her lip. She couldn't go into a tailspin every time Todd wasn't in school. Besides, hadn't Minda said she'd seen him earlier?

"Lexi, are you all right?" Mr. Raddis asked. "You look a little pale."

"Oh, yeah. Just not enough sleep, I guess." Lexi made a concerted effort to smile.

"Then you and the rest of the class are in luck," he said. "There's no danger of my putting you to sleep with a lecture. All classes are to go to the gymnasium this hour for a special presentation."

"What's it about?" someone asked.

"I have no idea. When I got the new schedule last week there was no mention of it."

"I hope it's not another one of those stupid demonstrations," Tressa complained.

"You mean like the one with all the reptiles and amphibians?"

"Gross."

"It's strange that no one knows what they're calling us to the gymnasium for."

"We'll find out shortly," Mr. Raddis said. "Everyone, to your feet. Let's go."

The halls were abuzz with students. Lexi searched for some sign of Todd. *Where* is *he*?

"Looking for Todd?" Binky said, edging closer to Lexi. The press of the crowd almost caused Binky to trip and fall. "What is your rush?" she asked the boy behind her. "Why is everybody so anxious to get to the gym, anyway?"

"They're not anxious to get to the gym," Egg

pointed out, "they're just glad to get out of class. There's a difference."

"What do you think it's about?" Lexi asked.

Egg shrugged his shoulders and pointed toward the empty gym. "There's no gear set up for a demonstration, just a podium."

Mrs. Waverly and Mr. Link, the principal, were standing next to the podium in the center of the room.

"Hey, there's Todd!" Binky said, pointing to a side door across the huge floor.

Lexi gasped. Todd was escorting Nancy into the gymnasium! They were walking toward Mrs. Waverly.

Mr. Link stepped to the podium, and the room quieted quickly. "Good morning. I'm sure you're all wondering why we called this meeting. We have a unique and special opportunity. Miss Nancy Kelvin has asked to speak to the students of Cedar River High today. Nancy is a nurse from our local hospital, specializing in pediatrics. She tells me this is her very first stop in a series of talks she has planned to present in schools about a compelling subject, of which she has firsthand information."

"Get *on* with it," Lexi heard Gina mutter. "Let her talk."

"Today Nancy will be speaking to us about AIDS."

There was a hum of vocal response to the announcement, and then silence. The students had already been bombarded with facts, figures, and statistics about AIDS.

"*More* about AIDS?" Tressa hissed. "I can't believe it! What does it have to do with us, anyway?"

"I don't know why they keep hammering it home," Minda added.

Just be quiet and listen, Lexi wanted to say. She sighed and leaned back against the wall. Nancy had warned her family she had some ideas up her sleeve. She certainly hadn't waited long to implement them.

The audience gave Nancy a round of applause as she moved to the podium. Out of the corner of her eye, Lexi caught Binky's questioning look. Lexi stared straight ahead.

"Hi everyone," Nancy began brightly. "I'm really glad to be here with all of you today." She made a face. "But I don't like podiums." She lifted the microphone from its stand and pulled a stool out from behind the podium. She settled herself on the stool only a few feet from the bleachers. She looked very much like an elf, what with her short dark hair, twinkling eyes, and small frame.

"She's cute," Tressa whispered. "Isn't she Mike Winston's girlfriend?"

"I think so," someone answered.

"Seems like she'd have a more interesting topic to talk about than AIDS."

Lexi thought Nancy's color was better today. She looked rested, and as usual, beautiful.

"As your principal told you, I am a nurse, and therefore qualified to talk to you about the subject of AIDS. But I'm not going to give you a lecture about what AIDS is and what it does to the immune system. I'm sure you've heard plenty about that from your capable teachers right here at Cedar River High. Rather, I'm going to talk about another aspect of the disease . . . as it particularly relates to teenagers.

"I know many of you are probably bored already, wondering how long this is going to take, and what in the world more I can say to you that you don't already know. The best part is that you don't have to be in class right now."

A chuckle rippled through the crowd. Lexi knew Nancy had captured her audience.

"You see, there's another very dangerous aspect to AIDS that no one pays much attention to, but we have to start paying attention—*soon*. Teenagers naturally have a feeling of . . . invincibility . . . They feel healthy. They're strong. They're young. What can happen? Right? They are reasonably smart, and they're convinced that AIDS, or any other sexually transmitted disease for that matter, can't touch them.

" 'That can only happen to so-and-so,' you might say. 'Someone who's stupid enough to indulge in premarital sex, or dumb enough to do drugs. AIDS will never touch me,' you say to yourself, feeling confident and smug.

"Well, I'm here to tell you that you're wrong. Dead wrong. You aren't invincible. You aren't safe from the danger of AIDS. *Unless* you make up your mind, right here and now. Unless you make a personal commitment, no exceptions, to wait for sex until you are married and in a monogamous relationship, and to never do drugs, you too could contract the HIV virus that causes AIDS."

Nancy's expression was so intense, several students in the front row shifted uneasily.

" 'Everybody's doing it' is one line I hear occasionally. Don't kid yourselves. Everyone's *not* doing it. At least, not the smart ones. Sex is not a teenage sport, contrary to popular opinion." There was a small ripple of laughter. "It's for married people, *only*. That's the way God intended it, and that's the only way it is safe and right.

"Maybe you look at a potential sex partner and say, 'There's nothing wrong with her, she looks healthy.' Or, 'I'll be safe with him, he hasn't slept with anyone else. He says he loves me.'

"Well, let me tell you something else. You can't tell by the way a person looks whether or not he has the AIDS virus."

Someone in the first row blurted, "I don't believe that. How could someone have AIDS and not look sick? Don't they get all pale and skinny?"

"Not right away. You can carry the virus for up to ten years before you get sick," Nancy answered.

Tressa's hand shot up. "There's nobody in Cedar River with AIDS. We would have heard about it."

"Okay," Nancy said. "Anyone else?"

"My parents say AIDS is a disease of gays. It seems to me you'd be safe if you weren't gay and you didn't hang around with them."

There was another buzz through the audience. Some of these questions sounded as though students hadn't been listening in health class.

"I thought you got AIDS in places like New York or Africa. Not Cedar River," someone said.

Lexi was impressed with how easily Nancy drew questions from the crowd. And no question caught her off guard.

A girl Lexi didn't know timidly raised her hand in the front row. "You said teenagers shouldn't have sex with anyone until they're married. But what if they're really in love and want to get married someday? If a guy looks and seems really nice, I don't see what the problem is . . ."

"Let's use your question as an example," Nancy said. "Let's say that a girl named Sue meets a boy she really likes. We'll call him Tim. Tim tells Sue he loves her. He's handsome and sharp-looking. He even comes from a good family. Sue has sex only with him. That's what we call a monogamous relationship. But there's a little problem here. Tim doesn't tell Sue that he has had other sex partners before he met her. Say, for example, he had two girlfriends before Sue. And those two girlfriends each had two boyfriends. Maybe those two boys—you get the picture. Sue is not just having sex with Tim. In reality she's having sex with Tim *and* the partners of his former partners. And the really sad part is that if only *one* person in that group of people has the AIDS virus, it is possible for Sue to get it, even if Tim shows no present signs of the disease."

The gymnasium was deathly quiet.

"*You can decide to have sex with one person, only one time, and that one time could kill you.* God intended for each of us to have just one mate and to be faithful to that mate for life. That's the only plan that works, that will keep us safe from AIDS. Of course, when you are contemplating marriage, you will have to be completely honest with each other. If there is a remote chance that one of you could have been exposed to the virus, testing should be done before you marry."

"Aren't you overdramatizing this just a little bit?" Tressa spoke up. "I can't believe that this can be such a problem in Cedar River."

"Maybe I *am* a little dramatic," Nancy admitted.

"But there's something I haven't told you. I may look healthy, and do live in Cedar River—but *I have AIDS*."

Lexi saw jaws drop all around her, and heard a few gasps. By and large the students sat in stunned silence, their eyes wide open. No one moved.

Nancy slid off the stool and walked back and forth in front of the bleachers. "Maybe you'd like to look at me a little closer. Do I look sick to any of you?"

"She's serious," Tressa whispered to Minda. "I can't believe she's serious."

"All those comfortable, preconceived notions you had about being safe here in Cedar River just aren't true. None of us are safe. And until we realize that and change our lifestyles, people are going to die.

"It was the most devastating moment of my life when the doctors told me that I had AIDS. It was as though I'd stepped into a bottomless pit. I felt like I was falling, falling, falling—and if I ever hit bottom, I'd be painfully, horribly smashed into a million pieces. I was hurt and angry. I asked, 'Why me? Why not someone else?'

"When I pulled myself together, I had to ask myself another question. 'Why *not* me?' I realized the decisions I made in the past, about eight years ago, had brought me to this. I became very sad. It was as though a part of me had already died. Certainly my hopes and dreams for the future had died. One moment I was planning my wedding, and the next I was thinking about my funeral."

Lexi glanced at Todd. His head was in his hands, and she knew he was sobbing.

"Then there was the awful job of telling my family and friends what was wrong with me." There were tears in Nancy's eyes now, threatening to spill over. "I have to thank God for my fiancé and his family because they have been so loving and supportive. I don't know what I would have done if they'd turned away from me. I'd already lost everything else. I was terrified that I would lose them too. But instead of showing fear and backing away from me, they embraced me and told me they still loved me. That was a beautiful gift.

"Think about it. If someone *you* knew had AIDS, or you'd heard a rumor that they did, how would you react? Would you keep your distance? If you came in contact with the person involuntarily, would you rush to wash your hands afterward? Or would you treat that person as a living, breathing, hurting individual who needed affection, love, and understanding?"

If anyone had been disinterested in Nancy's speech in the beginning, she now held them transfixed.

"I've recently decided what I want to do with the rest of my life. I want to warn teenagers—like you—about AIDS. I apologize if I'm not very skilled at getting my message across, but you are the first group I've spoken to. My friends and family didn't want me to do this so soon after leaving the hospital, but I knew I had to do it. I might not have much time left, and there are so many teenagers to warn.

"If you remember nothing else, remember this, *AIDS is preventable!*"

Binky raised her hand. "Can you tell us more about how we can be safe?"

"It's your choice. If you choose to be drug-free, have no premarital sex, and if you haven't had a medical problem that required a blood transfusion prior to 1985, you're not likely to ever contract the HIV virus. Another way to insure your safety is to abstain from the use of alcohol."

"What does alcohol have to do with AIDS?" someone asked.

"It doesn't have anything to do with it directly. But drinking alcohol lowers your inhibitions. People do things under the influence of alcohol that they would not normally do. The things you might try under its influence would terrify you if you were sober."

"What about when we do marry? What about sex then?" one of the Hi-Fives asked.

"It's important to be sure that you and your partner are healthy and free of the HIV virus, and that your relationship is a monogamous one—that means neither of you have other sexual partners. Some people insist on a blood test."

"That takes the romance out of things, doesn't it?" came a comment from someone at the back.

"Maybe, but AIDS has changed the way we live." Nancy's expression was melancholic. "I wish someone had come to my school when I was your age and told me what I'm telling you. It might have saved my life. It wasn't until I became a Christian that I realized how wrong and foolish I'd been, and changed my lifestyle."

Nancy's voice quavered with emotion. "If I could teach you anything, it would be to learn from my mistakes. Don't do what I did.

"My decision to come out publicly about my illness has been frightening and frustrating for my family and friends. It would have been much easier for me and them to keep my condition a secret. There would have been no stares, no questions, no fear. I can see it already in some of your faces. You don't want to be near me now. You're afraid. I'd like to have avoided that, but there isn't time. I don't know how long I'm going to feel well. It could be two weeks, or two years. I feel the urgent need to warn others.

"God intended sex to be a beautiful expression of love within the bonds of marriage. It still can be. Don't misuse the gift." Nancy paused, scanning her audience. "I've talked long enough. Thanks for listening. Be smart. Be safe."

The applause was deafening. The students rose to their feet, giving her a standing ovation, while the tears that had threatened to interrupt Nancy's speech finally coursed down her cheeks.

Some students left the gymnasium, most stayed where they were, but a few moved toward Nancy. Lexi patiently waited her turn as the students each tried to embrace Nancy or give her a word of thanks.

Minda wedged herself in front of Lexi. "Excuse me. I want to talk to her before she leaves."

Lexi stepped aside as Minda planted herself firmly in front of Nancy's chair. "You're really brave," Minda said. There was a genuine note of admiration in her voice.

"Not by myself," Nancy said with a gentle smile. "With God's help, and the support of my friends."

"Whatever. You're still brave. Thanks for coming. It made me think."

"That's what I'd hoped for."

Egg, Binky, and Jennifer hung back with Lexi until everyone else had left the gymnasium. Then Egg reached out, grabbed Nancy's hand and embraced her in a huge, bearlike hug.

"I'm not afraid anymore," he said softly.

"Me, either." There were tears in Binky's eyes. "I'm ashamed of how we acted the other night," she admitted. "I'd heard the rumor and we didn't understand how it could happen to you. As much as we'd heard about AIDS, it was scary to have it hit so close to home. It's about us. It's about people around us. I wasn't very sympathetic or forgiving before, but I'm going to be now."

The brave mask that Nancy had been wearing finally crumbled. She opened her arms to Binky, Egg, Jennifer, and Lexi. Lexi had cried so many times over Nancy's illness already, but now at least her tears were happier ones.

Chapter Eleven

"Does anyone know where my brother went?" Binky caught up with Lexi, Jennifer, and Peggy as they walked down the sidewalk after school.

"He and Todd were going to Mike's garage," Peggy said. "That's where we're headed. Want to come along?"

"I suppose so. There's nothing else to do." Binky kicked at a clump of dirt and sent it spinning off into the street.

"How's everything going?" Lexi inquired. Binky seemed abnormally quiet and introspective.

"Great. Harry sent me flowers yesterday. I think he's more crazy about me than ever." She grinned. "Amazing, huh?" Binky kicked at another clump of dirt. "It's just that I keep thinking about Nancy. Every time I get a happy thought, a sad one follows."

"I know what you mean," Lexi agreed. "No matter how hard I try, I can't seem to get her illness out of my mind, either."

When they arrived at the garage, Todd and Egg were sitting in Mike's office on two folding chairs, their feet propped up on Mike's desk. They were watching a golf tournament on an old black-and-white television set mounted on a shelf in the corner.

Jennifer plopped onto the torn vinyl couch and picked up an old magazine. "This looks like a lot of fun. I'm sure glad I came," she said sarcastically.

Ed walked into the room wiping his grease-stained hands on his coveralls. "What's this, a party?"

"We came to see what Todd and Egg were up to, but they're pretty much occupied." Lexi inclined her head toward the boys, who were glued to an instant replay.

"Want something to drink?" Ed asked. "My treat."

"You're in a good mood today," Peggy commented. "What's up?"

"Haven't you heard?" Egg removed his legs from the desk and dropped them to the floor. "Ed's got a girlfriend."

"No kidding!" Binky said. "Good for you! Anyone we know?"

Ed grinned from ear to ear and blushed pink. "She works out at the college."

"Ooooh, a college woman. How did you manage that?" Peggy asked.

Lexi couldn't help but smile as she watched her friends tease Ed. He'd changed so much since she'd first met him. He was confident, no longer ashamed to voice his own opinions.

"Ed's girlfriend is the literacy volunteer who's been teaching him to read," Egg offered. "Ed's been getting quite an education."

"You must be a quick learner, Ed," Jennifer remarked. "If you managed to impress your tutor enough to date you, that is."

"It's my innate charm," Ed shot back. "She

couldn't resist it." A grin split his face. "Did you notice the word I used?—innate. Are you impressed?"

When he'd first started working for Mike, Ed had been shy, almost hostile. He was so afraid someone would find out he couldn't read or write. Now that he was learning to do both, he'd conquered his insecurity and apparently managed to fall in love with his instructor.

"Do I hear wedding bells?" Todd put his hand to his ear.

"He's not denying it," Jennifer joked.

"You mean you're really serious about this girl, Ed?" Lexi asked. "When's the wedding?"

Ed grinned, and squirmed like a happy puppy. "Oh, I don't know. Nothing's for sure. Even if it works out, we wouldn't get married until after Mike and Nancy's—" As soon as the words were out, Ed realized what he was about to say. He was talking about a wedding that had been put on hold. Temporarily? Or forever?

Egg cleared his throat several times. "What are Mike and Nancy going to do now?" he asked Todd. "Are they still planning to get married?"

"Everything's in limbo for the time being."

Suddenly Todd saw Mike standing in the doorway. "How long have you been there?"

"Long enough to hear that Ed finally found himself a girl," Mike said weakly.

"Mike, I'm sorry. I didn't mean to—"

Mike slapped Egg on the back. "Don't feel bad, pal. It's a valid question. Lots of people have been wondering what Nancy and I are going to do now—including us. This AIDS thing has blown us out of the water. Nancy is determined to do as many public speaking presentations as she can while she feels well. She'll need all her energy for that."

"But where does that leave you?" Jennifer asked.

"When or if we marry, it will be a small family affair. Not the big celebration we first planned." Mike sighed. "I guess that's not all bad. I was dreading getting dressed up in a penguin suit and marching down the aisle, anyway. Funny, I thought a big wedding was the last thing I wanted. Now that we can't have it, I'm actually feeling cheated."

"This whole thing is a bummer, Mike." Peggy wrapped an arm around his shoulders.

Mike returned Peggy's gesture with a hug. "It is, no doubt about that. But we can't look back. All we can do is live one day at a time now. It may be that Nancy and I will decide not to get married at all. Her illness has changed everything for us, but I'll never stop loving her."

A small stir in the doorway prompted everyone to turn. Nancy stood there with a loving, tender look in her eyes. She walked wordlessly to Mike and embraced him.

"Thank you," Lexi heard her whisper.

"I don't know whether to laugh or cry," Jennifer blurted.

"Then laugh, Jennifer," Nancy said. "This is a great day. The sun is shining, I'm feeling well, and I know I'm loved."

Nancy's strength is awesome, Lexi thought. *But then,* she reminded herself, *she has tapped into the biggest power Source in the universe.*

Nancy put her hands on her hips. "Well, doesn't anyone want to know what I'm doing here?" she demanded. "I've got something simply wonderful planned!"

Chapter Twelve

"All right, what's up?" Todd stood and put his arm around Nancy.

"I'm on my way to visit one of my former patients."

"Isn't it hard going to the hospital now that you've quit your job?" Jennifer asked. Nancy had resigned from her nursing position as soon as she'd been diagnosed.

"I'm not going to the hospital."

"Where's your patient, then?" Binky asked.

"The baby was released into the care of a couple who take in foster children. Her mother is very sick."

"How sad. A baby who's not with her mom?" Binky asked sympathetically.

"Yes. But the foster mother loves company, and I'd like you all to meet her—and the baby. She's so beautiful . . ."

"Come on, Ed," Mike interrupted. "We've got work to do. See you, hon." He and Ed disappeared into the garage.

Nancy smiled. "Bye."

"Wouldn't this woman think it strange if you came to visit with six other people?" Binky asked.

"She'd love it. In fact, she says the one thing she

misses is not having teenagers at home anymore. You'll make her day. And we won't stay long."

"You've got something up your sleeve, Nancy," Todd said suspiciously.

"Why, Todd, when did you become a detective?" Nancy retorted.

Lexi knew Todd was right. With Nancy there was always a reason, a plan. But, as usual, there was no way Lexi could guess what it might be.

"Let's humor her, then," Lexi said. "Come on, let's go."

"How do you propose we all get there?" Jennifer protested.

"I've got my minivan." Nancy jingled her keys in front of Jennifer's nose. "We'll all fit nicely."

The house was in the oldest part of Cedar River. The trees were huge, almost forming an arch over the street. All the houses were small, with well-kept lawns.

"This looks like a cozy place," Peggy commented as they walked up the steps of the white bungalow with green shutters. "Like there could be chocolate chip cookies baking in the oven, and a pot of tea steeping on the table."

Nancy burst out laughing. "You've described it perfectly." She knocked on the front door while the others waited, slightly uncomfortable about this mysterious visit.

The lady who answered the door definitely belonged to the house. She was short and plump, with a bright smile and ruddy-pink cheeks. She seemed absolutely delighted that Nancy had come to visit with her teenaged friends.

As soon as they stepped inside, Lexi could smell

fresh-baked cookies and hear a teapot simmering on the stove. Peggy had been absolutely right.

"Cookies, anyone?" Mrs. Campbell asked, passing a large plate of chocolate chip cookies. No one could resist.

"How is Sammi today?" Nancy inquired.

"Growing like a weed. The little dear is getting such chubby cheeks, and oh my, how those little legs have grown!"

"Where is she?" Nancy asked. "I have to say hello to her."

"She's sleeping in her bassinet in the living room. Why don't you all go in and have a peek."

The living room was a cozy clutter of comfortable-looking chairs and sofas, with afghans, magazines, and books strewn about. In the center of the room was a white bassinet lined with fluffy, pink blankets. In it lay the most beautiful baby Lexi had ever seen. She was pink and round, with a button nose and long black eyelashes. The baby's mouth was so perfect, it appeared to be painted on in a little pink bow. Her lower lip trembled, and she stirred in her sleep.

"Look at her. She's gorgeous!" Binky exclaimed.

Egg stooped down to the bassinet. "And she snores!"

"That's not a snore." Binky punched her brother's shoulder. "It's a purr."

"You know, I think you're right for a change. She does sound like a kitten purring."

The infant's tiny fist lay close to her ear.

"Look at those fingers." Egg was transfixed. "They're perfect."

Mrs. Campbell stepped into the room. "She's a doll, that one, isn't she?" At the sound of a familiar voice, the baby's eyes fluttered open. She yawned widely and smacked her lips together in satisfied contentment.

When the baby stretched, arching her back, Jennifer cooed admiringly. All of them were smitten by the child's beauty.

"Did you say the baby's mother is sick?" Peggy asked. "She must feel terrible not being able to be with her new baby."

Nancy and Mrs. Campbell exchanged glances.

"Ellen—that's Sammi's mother's name—is in a drug treatment center," Mrs. Campbell said. There was a tinge of sadness in her voice.

"Drug treatment?" Binky sounded shocked. "You mean this baby's mother was taking drugs before the baby was born? How awful!"

"It's worse than that." Nancy stroked the downy hair on the baby's head. "Sammi has tested HIV-positive. She was infected at birth by her drug-addicted mother."

Jennifer and Peggy blanched. Binky looked like she might faint.

Egg and Todd stared at the baby, quiet fury written on their faces.

"But she's so innocent. So tiny. How unfair," Lexi said.

"Poor baby," Binky said softly. "You didn't do a thing to deserve this."

Suddenly everyone was very quiet. It seemed to dawn on them at once what Nancy was trying to show by this visit.

"AIDS is a disease, not a punishment from God," Nancy said simply. "It can touch innocent children like Sammi as well as her drug-addicted mother. Until we realize this, we won't treat victims of this disease with the compassion they need and deserve.

"As Christians, it is our responsibility to help those who are hurting, not pass judgment on them. Sick people are suffering. God doesn't tell us to be kind to those who contracted AIDS through blood transfusions, and ignore those who acquired it from shared needles, or illicit sex. As Christ's representatives we must show compassion and serve people unconditionally, just as He did."

"But maybe God is trying to tell us something . . ."

"It's true, Binky, that He certainly doesn't condone sex outside of marriage, or hurting our bodies with drugs. But why would He choose this point in time to tell us that through a disease? People have been sinning against their bodies since the beginning of time."

"Because people sin more now than they used to?" Binky guessed.

Nancy shook her head. "We've all sinned, Binky. There isn't anything new happening out there. You have to remember that because God is perfect, *all* sin is evil in His sight. Whether it's the 'white' lie, the small theft, or the gossip, it's all equally abhorrent in God's sight.

"If you believe that God sent AIDS to punish sexual sin, then where's the disease for people who cheat in school, rebel against their parents, or shoplift?

"Sin is all the same to Him. We simply cannot judge other people. That's His job."

"I'd be in trouble if there were a disease for people who gossiped," Binky said, shuddering.

"And aren't you glad you don't have the responsibility of judging others, Binky? Wouldn't you feel awful if it were your job to condemn others for their sins, when you knew what sins you were guilty of?"

Binky nodded. "You've convinced me, Nancy."

"AIDS is a natural result of human beings mistreating their own bodies. It is nature demanding a price. By being sexually irresponsible, a dangerous disease has spread all over the world. We should be blaming ourselves for what's happening, not God.

"Our country is beginning to pay for the so-called 'sexual revolution.' What was touted as freedom has reaped an awful price."

"But what can we do about it now?" Binky asked, looking sadly at the cooing infant.

"Educate people of the dangers, and then have compassion on those afflicted without pitying or judging them."

Mrs. Campbell picked up the baby and gently placed her in Lexi's arms. Lexi held her close and watched her yawn, then fix her eyes on Lexi. It made Lexi laugh lightly, until she realized tears were streaming down her own cheeks. She handed the child back to Mrs. Campbell.

"I'm a little confused," Lexi admitted. "That baby isn't bad because she has AIDS, and I'm not good because I don't."

Everyone had tears in their eyes and were at a loss for words, until the mood was broken by the sudden foghornlike sound of Egg blowing his nose.

Egg looked up, and everyone was smiling or laughing. "What's so funny?" he demanded.

"You're good for us, Egg," Lexi said. "We needed

you to get us to smile again."

But it was a somber bunch who said goodbye to Mrs. Campbell and Sammi, and made their way outside to Nancy's minivan.

Chapter Thirteen

Lexi met Binky at the front door of the Winston home. Binky was lugging a stack of books.

"Need help?" Lexi asked.

"Nah. I'm feeling great. I think I could move a mountain if I had to." Binky grinned. "I'm still proud of myself for standing up to Harry and telling him what I thought. It's made me feel strong. Besides, I know now that I couldn't have lived with myself if I'd gone ahead and stayed the weekend with him. Standing up for my beliefs has made me feel in control of my life. I like the feeling." As she entered the house, half the books she was carrying spilled onto the floor. "Of course, being in control of my life and being in control of these books are two different things . . ."

———

"Do you understand this stuff?" Egg complained some minutes later as he glared at his chemistry book. "What answer did you get for problem number four?"

"I didn't get *any* answer," Binky told him.

"Todd, you're the chemistry buff. You'll have to explain it to the rest of us."

"Do I look like Einstein?" Todd stuck a pencil behind his ear and leaned back in his chair to explain the problem.

Binky stared out the window, oblivious to everything around her until Lexi poked her.

"Did you get that answer?"

"Huh? Did someone say something? I guess I wasn't listening."

"What are you thinking about?" Lexi asked her.

"Mike and Nancy—again. What's going to happen next, Todd?"

Todd rolled his pencil across the table. "I don't know. They're taking one day at a time."

Binky looked so troubled that Todd almost laughed. "I know you've got another question rolling around in your head, so you might as well ask it."

"I don't want to make you feel bad or anything—"

"Spit it out, Binky."

"Will Nancy die soon of her disease? I mean, they must have told her something about how much time she has."

Lexi winced at Binky's question. She ached for Todd.

"Nobody really knows, Binky. It all depends on whether or not she gets some other disease that her body can't fight off. Anyway, Nancy refuses to dwell on it. She says it's not productive, and she wants to be positive and upbeat so she can help others.

"She's really brave. More brave than I could ever be," Todd continued. "But there's research being done every day. Who knows when something might be developed that will help Nancy."

"Are you talking about me again?"

Todd turned to see his brother and Nancy standing in the doorway.

Nancy walked over to Binky and put her hand on her shoulder. "I'd just like to tell you how sweet I think you are to be worrying about me as much as you do. But please don't worry anymore. It doesn't do any good."

"I can't help it, Nancy," Binky moaned. "I feel so bad for you and so helpless."

"I'm not going to ruin what I have by thinking about what I've lost." Nancy looked at Todd, Lexi, and their friends. "I have today; I have Mike; I have my family. I'm a pretty lucky girl, I'd say."

"But the wedding—" Lexi knew Binky couldn't resist bringing it up.

"Mike and I have postponed our wedding indefinitely. I have set so many goals for myself concerning AIDS education that both of us feel they should take first priority." She looked wistfully at Mike. "And frankly, it's probably not a good idea for Mike and me to be married. I don't want to risk infecting him with the HIV virus."

Binky blushed, and Nancy went on. "Other couples have taken precautions for safe sex when one of the partners is HIV-infected, but I'm not sure that's the right choice for us. I want Mike to be one-hundred-percent safe. My doctor and I are considering AZT, an AIDS treatment drug. There's hope that, while a cure for AIDS may not be found for a long time, we can learn to deal with it as a chronic illness. New facts are being learned every day. We're leaving our options open."

"How do you feel about that, Mike?" Egg asked cautiously.

"I'd rather be married," Mike admitted, "but Nancy is calling the shots on this. She has to feel comfortable too. Besides, she knows I still love her. That will never change."

"It must be hard to live with this every day, knowing that something is wrong inside your body and there's no way to stop it," Lexi said.

"It's hard, but not impossible," Nancy said with confidence. "My heavenly Father has forgiven me and cleansed me, and promised to be with me now and throughout eternity. He's given me today, and I thank Him for it. I want to enjoy it.

"In 1 Peter 2:24, it says, 'Christ carried our sins in his body on the cross. He did this so that we would stop living for sin and start living for what is right. And we are healed because of his wounds.'"

Egg watched Nancy's face as she spoke. Now he looked at Mike. "No wonder you love her."

Mike pulled Nancy in close and rested his head on hers. "She is wonderful, isn't she?"

Lexi looked around the room at her friends and realized afresh just how precious this day was. *Every day* was precious.

It had taken Nancy's illness to make Lexi recognize the fact.

———

Jennifer uncovers a secret that threatens to tear apart her family and her life in Cedar River. Read about it in *A Special Kind of Love*, book 21 in the CEDAR RIVER DAYDREAMS series.

A Note From Judy

I'm glad you're reading *Cedar River Daydreams*! I hope I've given you something to think about as well as a story to entertain you. If you feel you have any of the problems that Lexi and her friends experience, I encourage you to talk with your parents, a pastor, or a trusted adult friend. There are many people who care about you!

I love to hear from my readers, so if you'd like to receive my newsletter and a bookmark, please send a self-addressed, stamped envelope to:

Judy Baer
%Bethany House Publishers
11300 Hampshire Avenue South
Minneapolis, MN 55438